Bolan turned to see the terrorist collapse on the floor, a single bloody hole just above his left eyebrow. The cardboard box flew through the air, hit the floor and rolled to a stop in a pile of shattered pottery.

Footsteps sounded on the porch, then Platinov burst through the door, her H&K pistol held in a two-handed grip. The warrior beckoned, and she followed him to the box in a corner.

He brushed the broken pieces of earthenware to the side with his foot. Dropping to his knees, he reached out and set the box upright. A bullet hole, the edges scorched and brown, stared back at them from the cardboard.

Platinov held back a sob. "Is it the...?"

Bolan didn't answer. He opened the box and withdrew a long, metal cylinder. A dark green substance covered the side of the tube where the vacuum created by the round had brought some of the contents with it.

He looked into the cardboard box. The same substance dripped down the sides of the empty container. Bolan set the box on the floor and faced Platinov.

Neither spoke. Both knew they'd been exposed to the deadly virus.

MACK BOLAN®

The Executioner

DON PENDLETON'S
THE EXECUTIONER®
FEATURING MACK BOLAN®
COMBAT STRETCH

A GOLD EAGLE BOOK FROM
WORLDWIDE®

TORONTO • NEW YORK • LONDON • PARIS
AMSTERDAM • STOCKHOLM • HAMBURG
ATHENS • MILAN • TOKYO • SYDNEY

First edition August 1991

ISBN 0-373-61152-8

Special thanks and acknowledgment to
Jerry VanCook for his contribution to this work.

COMBAT STRETCH

Government and cooperation are in all things
the laws of life; anarchy and competition,
the laws of death.
>   —John Ruskin
>   1819–1900

The time has come to put aside petty differences,
distrust and hatred. When the world faces a major
threat, only survival counts.
>   —Mack Bolan

THE
MACK BOLAN®
LEGEND

Nothing less than a war could have fashioned the destiny of the man called Mack Bolan. Bolan earned the Executioner title in the jungle hell of Vietnam.

But this soldier also wore another name—Sergeant Mercy. He was so tagged because of the compassion he showed to wounded comrades-in-arms and Vietnamese civilians.

Mack Bolan's second tour of duty ended prematurely when he was given emergency leave to return home and bury his family, victims of the Mob. Then he declared a one-man war against the Mafia.

He confronted the Families head-on from coast to coast, and soon a hope of victory began to appear. But Bolan had broken society's every rule. That same society started gunning for this elusive warrior—to no avail.

So Bolan was offered amnesty to work within the system against terrorism. This time, as an employee of Uncle Sam, Bolan became Colonel John Phoenix. With a command center at Stony Man Farm in Virginia, he and his new allies—Able Team and Phoenix Force—waged relentless war on a new adversary: the KGB.

But when his one true love, April Rose, died at the hands of the Soviet terror machine, Bolan severed all ties with Establishment authority.

Now, after a lengthy lone-wolf struggle and much soul-searching, the Executioner has agreed to enter an ''arm's-length'' alliance with his government once more, reserving the right to pursue personal missions in his Everlasting War.

Prologue

An electric charge of fear shot through Dr. Toshiro Takahata. He stared, spellbound, at his watch. In fifteen minutes he'd know.

Takahata opened the steel door to the lab and peered inside. At the far side of the room, her back to the door, his assistant, Junko Tamano, was busily washing dirty test tubes. He stood quietly, watching the woman. He'd been blessed to find such an enthusiastic protégée at this point in his career—when the aches and pains of advancing age had begun to prohibit some of the tasks he'd taken for granted as a younger man.

The old man smiled, the warmth of gratitude flooding his soul. Whatever the catalyst for her dedication, he was lucky to have found someone like Junko—young, and willing to accept the loneliness that accompanied her position in this secluded research outpost.

Takahata took a step forward, and Junko turned suddenly, pivoting on the balls of her feet and spinning smoothly to face him. Her hands rose in a classic karate posture, and an uncharacteristic ruthlessness twisted her features.

The gratitude in his heart turned to surprise. Takahata frowned. He hadn't been aware that she had trained in the martial arts. "I'm sorry," he apologized. "I've frightened you."

Slowly Junko lowered her arms. The scowl softened. She shrugged. "It's nothing. I just get jittery sometimes. We're so alone."

Takahata nodded. He paused uncomfortably, then stared at the clock on the wall. "It's almost time. Nine minutes."

"Yes. Perhaps this time we...*you* will have been successful."

Takahata crossed the room, taking the woman's hands in his as the fraternal bond returned. "*We* is correct, Junko. I could no longer function without your assistance." Dropping her hands, he shuffled slowly to a table at the center of the room and pulled a sterilized petri dish from the steel autoclave. Opening the lid with one hand, he took the inoculating needle from Junko with the other.

Takahata poured hot agar into the petri dish and watched as the liquid began to cool and harden. Expertly he scraped the needle back and forth across the gelatinous substance. "We'll pray for success," he said. "But, once again, we must prepare for failure."

The old man covered the dish and sat down at his desk while Junko returned to the sink. He glanced again at his watch. The memory of the ten-year-old peasant girl he'd seen only last week, her red-spotted body jerking spasmodically, returned to his mind like a flashback of a horror movie.

Typhus. Thousands of his fellow Japanese, as well as thousands more in other countries, continued to die each year from the microorganisms transmitted by lice and fleas. A vaccine was available, but it was expensive and hard to come by for the masses.

It had been the horror of typhus that had launched his campaign to isolate the disease's DNA and eradicate the disease. He had succeeded, but the cure had proved to be more deadly than typhus itself.

Takahata felt beads of perspiration break out on his forehead and pulled a rumpled handkerchief from his pocket. The virus he had inoculated into the agar had quickly killed the bacteria. But then, overnight, the bacteria had returned, combining with its attacker to create a horrifying, mutant substance the like of which he'd never seen. The potential for destruction was so great that he'd entrusted the knowledge to no one but Junko.

Since the occurrence of the mutation, the cure for typhus had taken a back seat to what Takahata now recognized as his responsibility—to rid the world of the monster he had created.

A vaccine to immunize had come quickly—a simple restructuring of the balance of virus to bacteria had proved to be an effective immunization. But finding an antitoxin—a cure for the disease once it had been contracted—had been far more difficult.

Six months of recombinate DNA experimentation had proved fruitless.

Takahata mopped the sweat from his brow and glanced toward the closed door that hid the glass isolation cage. In the cage Shiraga, the rat he had inoculated with his latest attempt at an antitoxin, would either be alive or dead. If he lived, then the cure had been discovered.

If Shiraga was dead, they had nothing but hope.

Takahata rose slowly, shuffled across the room and opened the door. Across the room, past the other cages filled with rats, guinea pigs and a lone chimpanzee, he saw the glass, and behind it the metal feed and water bins. Shiraga was nowhere to be seen.

Knees and back cracking loudly in the narrow confines of the room, Takahata moved to the glass, unclasped the latch and swung open the door. His fingers moved slowly into the cage. Behind the water bin he felt the cold, hard body.

Tears filled the old man's eyes as he closed the door and returned to the lab. Junko looked up from the sink long enough to see his pain before dropping her gaze once more.

Takahata returned to his desk and sat down, slowly leaning forward to bury his face in crossed arms. He fought against the depression that surged through his soul. The old man barely heard the knock at the door behind him. He didn't move. Somewhere, as if from far away, he heard Junko slide across the tile and open the door.

Takahata looked up as new footsteps neared. Through his bleary, tear-filled eyes he saw a half-dozen ski-masked men point machine guns at him. At his side Junko Tamano pressed an automatic pistol against his temple. The ruthlessness he'd seen in her face earlier had returned.

As if in a dream, Takahata heard his assistant say, "Doctor Takahata, I'd like to introduce Ichiro Musashi."

A short, stocky man with the build of a weight lifter pulled a stocking cap from his face. He stepped forward, his hand resting on the hilt of one of the three swords at his belt.

"What...what do you want of me?" Takahata asked.

A mirthless smile appeared on Musashi's face. "Why, to continue the work you have begun, Doctor," he said mockingly. "To continue the work you have begun."

1

Shattering the stillness of the dark mountain night, the first volley of shots tore across the hood of the Bronco. The second took out the windshield and both front tires.

Mack Bolan's foot shot reflexively to the brake, and both hands gripped the steering wheel as the Bronco scraped along the mountain wall. Metal shrieked and sparks flew through the darkness as the trim ripped away from the door.

As he fought the wheel, the Bronco's grille crashed into an outcropping of rock, reversing the spin of the vehicle and sending it spinning away from the mountain—toward the four-hundred-foot drop on the other side of the road.

Submachine gun fire seemed to erupt from all sides as the Bronco whirled to a halt, inches from the edge. Through the shattered glass of the windshield, Bolan saw the lights of the village far below. He pushed down on the door release, but the lever had jammed. Sliding across the seat, he wrenched open the passenger door and dived from the vehicle.

Bolan hit the ground, hearing the distinctive sound of a LAW as the rocket whined past. A split second later the Bronco exploded in flames. The force of the blast lifted him three feet off the ground and hurled him to the center of the highway. The warrior landed on his shoulder and rolled to his feet. He sprinted ahead to the cover of the mountain wall. His head rang from the concussion, and he felt the sticky warmth of blood trickling down his cheeks.

Muzzle-flashes winked on the ridge overhead, and behind the weapons Bolan could make out three shadows. Across the highway, just to the Executioner's right, was a two-foot opening between the mountain wall and a large boulder. He angled toward it, instinctively zigzagging as bullets kicked up dirt at his feet.

One slug seared across the top of his forearm, slicing neatly through the flesh above his wrist before speeding past the elbow. A second round streaked through the left chest pocket of his light sport coat. A blaze of pain stabbed across his rib cage as the round glanced off the Beretta 93-R and screamed across his skin, exiting through the rear of the jacket.

Ten feet from the opening in the rocks, the Executioner dived to the ground and slid the rest of the way. Then he sprang to his feet and twisted into the narrow opening.

The gunfire halted immediately. The warrior pressed his back against the rock wall, took a deep breath, then shrugged out of his jacket to examine his injuries. Both wounds were shallow. The bullet across his forearm had missed both the wrist and elbow. Bolan unknotted his necktie and wrapped it around the gash.

Deep crimson seeped through his white shirt where the second round had ricocheted off the Beretta, and the spot below the shoulder rig where the bullet had driven the hard steel into his flesh felt tender. Small fragments of plastic fell from the grip of the 93-R as he shifted the weapon. The double-stacked magazine peeked through the hole in the butt. Otherwise the Beretta still appeared serviceable.

The Executioner raised the Desert Eagle and traced the ridge as he waited for the next assault. Briefly he wondered who the men above him were, then pushed the question from his mind. Survival came first. Questions could wait.

A shadow appeared at the edge of the ridge, and Bolan squeezed the trigger of the .44. Tiny rocks and gravel cascaded over his head. An Ingram MAC-10 dropped onto the highway in front of him, followed a moment later by a body dressed in black fatigues.

The Executioner tightened his grip on his weapon as he sensed more movement overhead. He squinted into the darkness. Footsteps sounded, and two shadows inched forward. They ducked back again as gravel from under their boots slid over the side and fell to the road.

The warrior waited. Time ticked away, the seconds turning to minutes. The burning eased in his side, turning to a dull, distant ache. Finally another shadow edged over the side of the ridge. Bolan fired, and the shadow jumped back from view.

The Executioner took a deep breath. Of the three original gunmen, one lay dead on the road. A few minutes earlier the other two had shown themselves, still on the ridge. But this time it had been a lone shadow creeping toward the edge.

Where had the third gunman gone? Either he was still above, out of sight, or making his way down some unknown path in the rocks to catch the Executioner unaware.

Bolan scanned the immediate area. A row of pine trees bordered the cliff on the other side of the highway, their heavy bottom limbs drooping to the ground. The thickly needled branches would never stop bullets, but they'd offer concealment.

And they might be his only alternative.

An Uzi stuttered to his right, a long burst of slugs bouncing off the rock wall next to his head. Driven from behind the boulder, Bolan fired two quick shots in the direction of the muzzle-flash and sprinted back to the middle of the highway. More autofire assaulted him from behind, and he turned to fire twice more at the ridge overhead.

The Executioner turned and sprinted back across the highway. A short, tingling shiver ran down his spine as he *felt* the Uzi sights somewhere between his shoulder blades. Instead, the rounds rained over his head and to the sides as he passed the Bronco. Ten feet from the trees, he twisted, snap-shooting another .44 Magnum round to drive the man on high ground back from the edge. Then, firing one more time down the road into the darkness, he slid through the low limbs to the tree trunk.

He cast a quick glance to the rear. Three paces back the world ended, dropping four hundred feet to the abyss below. He turned back to the road. Through the dense branches he could see both the ridge and the highway.

Twenty yards down the highway a dark form stole forward, hugging the mountain wall. Bolan waited as the man inched closer.

Suddenly the shadow on the ridge reappeared, silhouetted against the sky. The gunman fired a scattered burst into the trees, trying to pinpoint Bolan's position for his partner before falling forward on his face.

The Executioner sighted down the barrel of the Desert Eagle, resting the front sight on the spot where the gunman had stood. Then, lowering the barrel a fraction of an inch, he squeezed the trigger and rolled away from the tree.

The high-pitched scream on the ridge echoed through the mountains. Then splinters of bark and sap flew from the tree trunk in front of the Executioner as the man on the ground fired at the Desert Eagle's muzzle-flash. Bolan continued his roll. He felt his feet drop over the edge of the cliff and threw both arms around the next tree in the row. Hoisting himself to a squat, he shoved a fresh magazine into the .44 and peered over his shoulder. The deadly drop-off was less than a foot behind him.

From his new position, the man on the highway was nowhere to be seen. Bolan leaned against the tree, straining to pick up any sound of the approach. Birds fluttered at the tops of the trees, searching for their own sanctuary away from the echoes of gunfire.

Silence.

The third gunman was taking his time. While he might not have pinpointed Bolan's exact position, he knew the man he hunted was somewhere in the line of trees—he could be nowhere else. His prey hadn't reappeared to the front.

Bolan glanced behind him again. And he wasn't going anywhere that way.

The gunman had restricted his movements to right and left. Or had he?

The Executioner looked up. The tree in front of him grew crookedly skyward, the trunk splitting ten feet above with the larger section angling out over the cliff.

Holstering the Desert Eagle, he rose and sprang upward, grasping a branch above his head. Chinning up and over the limb, he rose to his knees, clutching the trunk for balance. Slowly, branch by branch, he pulled himself higher into the air, gradually working outward until he was perched twenty feet in the air and six over the edge of the drop-off.

The limbs were sparser now, and through the twigs and needles Bolan saw his pursuer, who was dressed in black fatigues and ski mask like the gunman who'd dropped from the ridge. The man made his way along the edge of the trees, an Uzi gripped in his fists.

Bolan drew the Beretta from shoulder leather. He centered the front sight on the gunman's chest, then hesitated. He needed to take the man alive, needed to question him, find out who he was, and what the hell he was doing. Even more important, he needed to ascertain from where the leak had come.

The Executioner kept the sights on the gunman as the shadowy figure moved closer. Bolan would wait on the man and hope to get the drop on him once he was under the tree.

The man with the Uzi was fifteen feet away when the sparrow over Bolan's head chirped and flapped from the pine. The gunman's head jerked toward the noise, followed by the Uzi. The subgun jerked again, lowering to the Executioner's position as the masked man spotted him in the tree.

Aiming low, Bolan squeezed the trigger, drilling a lone 9 mm round into the masked man's abdomen, hoping to wound the man rather than kill him. The gunman stumbled back, the Uzi falling to arm's length at his side. Then the subgun barrel rose once more. The Executioner fired again, the next round crashing into the gunman's chest and dropping him to one knee.

Slowly the man in the black fatigues pressed the Uzi's extended stock against his shoulder and aimed once more for the tree. This time the Beretta 93-R spit a 3-round burst through the ski mask.

Carefully Bolan eased himself along the branch and back over the edge before dropping to the ground. He walked slowly to the body under the tree. Slinging the Uzi over his shoulder, Bolan pulled the ski mask from the mangled features. In the right-hand pocket of the black fatigue pants he found a key ring.

The Executioner walked to the highway and pulled the MAC-10 from under the man who had fallen. He squatted, pulled the mask above the second gunman's forehead and frowned. Returning to the crack between the boulder and mountainside, he threw his sport coat over his shoulders.

It took five minutes to climb the wall to the ridge where the last body lay cold in the dust. Bolan walked to the corpse. In the bright glow of the moon he saw that his blind round had entered the top of the man's head as the gunner had hugged the ground in false security. Bolan ripped the ski mask from the face, finding what by now he'd known he'd find.

All three men were Orientals.

BOLAN COULD SEE the Toyota parked a quarter of a mile up the road. As he walked toward the vehicle, he mentally replayed the conversation he'd had with Johnny earlier that day, searching for clues as to who might be behind the ambush.

Bolan's brother had answered their secure line on the second ring. "Brognola just called," he'd said without introduction. "It's urgent."

"What's the word?"

"The Man wants to see you."

"Did Hal say where?"

Johnny had gone on to relay the elaborate directions the big Fed from the Justice Department had given him to the cabin near the top of Backbone Mountain in the Blue Ridges.

Bolan jammed the key into the ignition before leaning over to open the glove compartment. Again he found what he'd expected. The car had been rented in nearby Hagerstown in the name of Sekichi Kawakami. Folding the papers, the Executioner stuffed them into the back pocket of his slacks. Brognola, when he found him, could run the name and Social Security number through NCIC.

For what good it would do. The odds were a thousand to one that Kawakami was anything other than an alias.

The Executioner started the engine and pulled the Toyota onto the twisting mountain road. Somewhere, either in the Justice Department or the White House itself, there was already a leak in the operation.

Whatever the operation was. He still didn't know.

Bolan shifted his shoulder rig as he climbed the mountain road. The bleeding on his forearm had stopped, and the injury to his ribs had turned out to be little more than an irritation. He'd been lucky.

The real pain came from beneath the holster, where the 9 mm parabellum had driven the Beretta into his side. Bolan switched on the overhead light, shifting the holster slightly to peer beneath the leather. The skin was bright red in the car light and had already begun bruising to a bright purple around the edges. He took a deep breath, and the pain intensified with the movement.

This unexpected attack would force him to alter his approach. What should have been a simple matter of driving up a mountain to a prearranged meeting place was about to become a delicate, tactical maneuver.

For all he knew at this point, the President could be captive...or dead.

Regardless, there was a leak *somewhere,* and he had to wonder whether it had really been Brognola that Johnny had talked to. His little brother had had limited contact with the Justice man in the past, and a good fake might have fooled him.

Bolan continued up the winding road. As he rounded yet another curve, the road moved away from the cliff, the mountain gradually extending out to his right. A moment later he passed a dark, deserted side road that led out onto a finger of the mountain.

A simple white sign marked the corner: Property of the United States Government. Authorized Personnel Only Beyond This Point.

This sign had been a landmark, a reference point Brognola had given Johnny to mark his turn. The directions called for Bolan to turn onto the dirt path and drive slowly. He'd eventually be met by Secret Service agents who would escort him to the cabin.

But the Executioner decided not to risk being ambushed again. For the time being he couldn't afford to trust anyone.

He drove a half mile farther before he spotted the scenic turnoff and pulled in beside the coin-operated telescope. He had no idea what he was about to face, but his plan more than likely would call for stealth, speed and agility rather than massive firepower. He had the Beretta and Desert Eagle. The Uzi and MAC-10 slung around his neck would just slow him down.

Cramming the weapons under the seat, Bolan covered them with his coat, exited the vehicle and jogged back down the highway toward the side road. Halfway there, he saw headlights round a curve, and ducked quickly into a grove of hardwoods.

As the lights neared, he made out the lines of a pickup truck. The vehicle drew alongside, and Bolan could make out the shadowy outlines of fishing gear and ice chests in the bed. A moment later it disappeared around another curve.

The warrior kept to the side of the road, taking advantage of any cover that presented itself. Two more vehicles—an ancient Volkswagen bus followed by a camper van—passed as he watched from behind a billboard.

Reaching the side road, Bolan dropped to his knees behind the U.S. Government sign. Out of sight down the road he heard the faint hum of a large car engine. As the noise grew louder, the dark lines of a Ford sedan appeared in the shadows. Bolan dropped to the ground.

Headlights dark, the blue sedan reached the intersection in front of him and braked. Bolan saw three whip antennae extending from the hood and trunk and caught a glimpse of the man riding shotgun—Caucasian—wearing an off-white trench coat. The car pulled past him onto the highway, made a U-turn and headed back in the direction it had come.

The Executioner rose from the ground and made his way through the undergrowth, following the road. Three antennae. The car had Secret Service written all over it. Either the agents in the car were authentic, or someone was going to great lengths to make them appear that way.

A hundred yards down the road the corner of an eight-foot chain-link fence popped into view. The side of the fence extended farther along the narrow finger of mountain, gradually fading into the darkness toward the cliffs.

The front of the fence ran parallel to the road. Dropping to the ground once more, the Executioner crawled forward through the grass. A moment later he saw the entrance gate, and behind it a guard shack. Two jeeps sporting .50-caliber machine guns had been parked on the gravel drive, and six armed and uniformed men leaned against the closed gate, talking and laughing. Two more did the same in the light of the guard shack. Behind the men, on the other side of the fence, a carefully sculptured hedge shielded the grounds behind from further view.

One of the guards at the gate cupped his hands, and in the soft mountain breeze Bolan heard the roll of a lighter wheel beneath his thumb. Flame sprouted, illuminating the man's face.

Moving closer still, the muffled conversations of the men drifted to him on the wind. Bolan listened. It was all in English—American-accented English.

It was beginning to look as if the situation at the cabin was just what he'd been told—the President and Brognola *were* there, awaiting his arrival. But there was still no proof, and now wasn't the time to start taking chances.

Slowly, drawing on instincts and battle sense that had become second nature over the years, Bolan surveyed the situation. The fence was too high to scale without being seen and, friend or foe, the guards at the gate would challenge him before he'd made it halfway up.

The side of the fence might lead anywhere. And more perimeter guards were bound to be stationed along its length, particularly if the President was there.

If he chose that path, there was always the possibility they'd spot him first.

The Executioner reached into his pocket. He'd take his chances with the devil he knew.

Edging slowly to the fence, he listened for sounds of movement from the men only thirty feet away. He unfolded the swivel base of the Leatherman Pocket Multi-Tool and opened the needle-nosed pliers, exposing the wire cutters. He glanced briefly at the fence, wondering if it might be electrified, then one of the guards answered the question.

Bolan held his breath, waiting, while the uniformed man walked toward him. The guard stopped five feet away to unzip his pants before urinating through the chain. Had the fence been "hot" the guard's water would have acted as a painful conduit. He glanced at the uniform as the man rezipped his trousers—U.S. Marines.

When the Marine had returned to his comrades, the Executioner went to work. The Leatherman hadn't been designed for such heavy-duty cutting, and it took the better part of five minutes to work through the first length.

A half hour later he'd opened enough wire to squeeze under. The moment of truth had arrived. While he wormed under the barrier, he'd be defenseless. And the Executioner knew all too well that men chosen to guard the President of the United States would take no chances. If they spotted him, they'd shoot first, saving any questions that crossed their minds for later.

Bolan rolled onto his back. He was about to begin when he heard the sedan coming back up the road. He froze, waiting. The engine slowed to an idle as the car pulled up in front of the guard shack. Two of the Marines vaulted the metal gate and walked to the road.

As the two men in uniforms talked to the men in the car, Bolan shot a last look at the rest of the guards. Their attention was completely focused on the blue sedan. He wouldn't get a better chance.

The Executioner slid under the fence, stood, then disappeared into the hedge on the other side. He made his way through the dense shrubbery until he spotted a lone man, tall and broad-shouldered, who sat at an umbrellaed picnic table. The man faced away from the Executioner and was reading a magazine by the light of an eight-cell police flashlight that rested on the table next to a walkie-talkie.

Silently Bolan moved from the hedge toward the preoccupied man. As he drew behind, Bolan looped a forearm around the man's throat, pressing the radial bone of his wrist against the windpipe. His other hand moved smoothly under the jacket, beating his opponent to the SIG-Sauer 9 mm pistol in shoulder leather.

The warrior's opponent was well trained. Throwing his weight forward, he grasped the flashlight and swung it backward over his shoulder.

Bolan dodged just in time, taking the blow meant for his head on the shoulder. The flashlight fell onto the grass. The Executioner dropped the SIG to the ground and pressed his other arm against the back of the man's head in the classic "sleeper" hold.

The man was strong as he grappled against the unexpected attack, but not strong enough. Bolan retained the hold until the body went limp, then eased the man to the ground.

The Executioner wasted no time. Relieving the man of everything but his underwear, he slipped out of his battle-soiled sport coat and donned the dark blue suit. He found a credential case in the inside coat pocket and, lifting the flashlight, he studied the Secret Service ID. The mustachioed picture appeared to match the face on the ground, which meant nothing. An organization that could set up the ambush at the bottom of the mountain would be more than capable of acquiring top-notch forgeries.

Bolan rolled the man over and bound his wrists behind him with a necktie. He ripped the sleeve from his sport coat, fashioned a crude gag and dragged the unconscious body into the hedge. Killing the flashlight, the Executioner pocketed the small walkie-talkie and moved across the garden.

An open courtyard was on the other side of the hedge, and in the center sat a rough stone, two-story cabin. Beyond the building the mountain dropped once more to the valley below.

Two more blue sedans, complete with whip antennae, were parked in the drive that led from the gate. To the left of the house a helicopter rested on the helipad, and Bolan could make out the presidential seal on the windshield.

He ducked back as a man in a trench coat approached from the left. As the guy came closer, Bolan saw an Uzi cradled in his arms. Moonlight bounced off the crown of the partially bald head as the gunner approached.

Bolan waited until the man came abreast, then reached through the leaves and ripped the Uzi from his grasp. A sharp gasp escaped the startled lips. The warrior pressed the subgun against the man's jaw, preventing further noise, then dragged him into the hedge.

Unknotting the tie from the unconscious man, the Executioner used the Leatherman to cut it in half. He bound and gagged the gunner, then searched him, finding Secret Service credentials and a SIG-Sauer. The man wore a nylon ankle holster, as well. Bolan ripped away the Vector retaining strap and found a Colt Agent .38 with a hammer shroud.

He slipped into the trench coat and shoved the Colt into the front pocket. The shroud would prevent the hammer from getting hung up on the material, allowing the gun to be fired through the coat from within the pocket, if necessary.

Staying behind the hedge and out of sight, Bolan circled the cabin, peering through the leaves and twigs. He saw four more men with Uzis, patrolling the perimeter of the cabin.

There were bound to be even more guards, but they would be scattered around the periphery of the grounds. With the exception of these four, and whoever waited inside, they should all be behind him now.

The Executioner stepped from behind the hedge and walked toward the cabin. Through the shadows, thirty yards away at the corner of the house, one of the men with the Uzis turned to watch.

Keeping one hand on the Colt in his pocket, Bolan raised the other in a casual salute, blocking his face in the shadows. He strode boldly toward the back door. The man waved back, then turned toward the front of the house.

Bolan walked to the back door, twisted the knob and stepped inside to a small laundry room. The door led to a hall, and he walked swiftly, passing a kitchen in which several white-clad men busied themselves at the sink and counters.

Low conversation drifted from the living room, and as he neared, Bolan recognized Brognola's voice. He relaxed slightly. It looked as if the cabin was secure.

Suddenly, from what appeared to be a bedroom, a man in his shirtsleeves stepped into the hall. He looked up at Bolan in surprise, which turned to shock as he focused on the Executioner's unfamiliar face. His hand shot toward the Smith & Wesson Model 19 holstered at his hip.

Bolan stepped forward and knocked the man against the doorjamb with his shoulder. He brought his right hand up, raising the coat-covered gun and jamming the hard steel barrel into the startled guard's abdomen.

"Take a good guess as to what's in the coat," he whispered.

The man nodded, his face taut.

Bolan pulled the weapon from the man's holster and pressed it into his back. Using the Model 19 as a prod, he pushed the man down the hall.

Just before they reached the living room, the dedicated agent made his play. Twisting suddenly, he brought his arm back in a vicious chop at Bolan's gun hand.

The Executioner stepped back, letting the chop glide by in front of him. He raised his left hand, blocking the other man's follow-up punch, and laid the Smith & Wesson across the agent's temple. The big agent dropped to the hall floor.

Bolan stepped over him and shoved the revolver into his belt. His hand still clutching the Colt in his coat pocket, he stepped into the living room.

Far across the spacious room the President, Brognola and another man sat facing one another in leather armchairs next to a roaring fireplace. As though sensing a presence, the three men turned to face the Executioner.

An expression of surprise crossed the President's face. He looked from Bolan to Brognola as the Justice man said, "Striker..."

All three men stood. The President extended his hand. "It's good to see you again, Mack. But as a matter of curiosity, where are Greg and Morris?"

"Who?"

"My bodyguards. The Secret Service agents who met you on the road."

Bolan shook his head. "I decided it might be wiser to come in alone."

The President raised his eyebrows. "You mean you made your way here without being spotted?"

"Let's just say, without being detained."

Without speaking the President strode to the picture window next to the fireplace. Cupping his hand around his eyes, he pressed his face against the glass and peered into the darkness. Then, walking slowly back to the center of the room, he looked at Brognola.

The Justice man grinned. "You knew he was good."

2

Bolan took a chair in front of the fireplace next to Brognola. The President and the tall, slender man resumed their seats facing them.

The President put a hand on the shoulder of the man next to him. "Striker," he said, "I'd like you to meet Doctor Rheinhold von Studnitz. Doctor von Studnitz is the chief virologist with the American Foundation for Viral Research."

Von Studnitz's gunmetal eyeglasses slid down the bridge of his nose as he leaned forward. He shook Bolan's hand before pushing the spectacles back against his forehead and reaching for a briar pipe in the lapel pocket of his coat. "It's a pleasure to meet you, Mr.... Striker?"

"Belasko will do."

The President twisted in his chair and lifted a phone from the end table next to him. "Prescott, find Hart and Cwayna." He turned to Bolan. "Now, Mack, if you don't mind..."

Bolan explained briefly about the ambush. Both Brognola's and the President's eyebrows rose slightly when he told them all three would-be assassins had been Oriental.

The President nodded. "I think the significance of the men's race will become clear to you shortly." He turned toward von Studnitz. "Doctor," he said, "I'll begin, then I'd like you to take over. We're running against the clock, and I want to get right to the point. You can explain the technical areas of this situation more efficiently than I can."

The doctor nodded. He jammed his pipe into a leather pouch, then tapped tobacco into the bowl with his forefinger as the President went on.

"A few months ago a Japanese research virologist named Toshiro Takahata was attempting to use some kind of virus to kill typhus bacteria. He had hoped to create a more efficient vaccine for the disease. Rather than kill the bacteria, however, the virus somehow combined with it." The President paused, pulled a white handkerchief from his pant pocket and gingerly dabbed at his forehead. "To make a long story short, Doctor Takahata developed a deadly new disease."

"A disease that spreads more easily than the common cold," von Studnitz added. He clenched the pipe between his teeth, thin trails of smoke escaping from both corners of his mouth. "Water, wind, apparently almost anything will transmit this viral-bacteria. Direct contact isn't necessary. The false fears the world has about the spread of AIDS—kissing, touching, mosquitoes—all pale by comparison to what has now been named Viral-Typhus, or Viryphus, if you will." Von Studnitz removed the pipe from his mouth. "At this time there's no cure, and I can't overemphasize what I'm about to say, Mr. Belasko. If Viryphus gets loose, it will mean the end of civilization as we know it within two years." He sat back in the chair, pausing to let the magnitude of his words sink in.

Bolan nodded. "The problem's obvious. If it falls into the wrong hands—"

Brognola broke in. "It already has."

"Takahata has been kidnapped by terrorists," the President added. "Terrorists well-known to us all—the Japanese Red Army. They've forced him to create a massive stock of Viryphus."

Bolan looked at von Studnitz. "The President said all this began a few months ago. Why didn't Takahata simply destroy the disease as soon as he realized what he'd created?"

Von Studnitz smiled sadly. "I'm sure with the advantage of his present hindsight he regrets not doing just that. But I've been acquainted with Doctor Takahata for years, and I think I can tell you with complete certainty what his thinking at the time must have been. If *he* had stumbled onto the disease, Takahata had to assume that someday someone else would, as well. He chose, as I would have, to study Viryphus and attempt to develop an antitoxin as insurance against that day."

Bolan looked at Brognola. "Where has all this information come from?"

The big Fed sat back in his chair and crossed his legs. "From the top terrorist himself, Striker." The Justice man glanced at von Studnitz. "Tell him, Doctor."

Von Studnitz chewed on his pipe stem. "I just returned from a small private island in the Ryukyus, Mr. Belasko. Top bacteriologists and virologists from around the world had been invited to what we thought was a research conference. But when we had assembled for the opening ceremony, a man unknown to us took the microphone. He introduced himself as Ichiro Musashi, the leader of the Japanese Red Army.''

He drew on his pipe before continuing. ''Men armed with machine guns suddenly appeared onstage and at the exits. Dr. Takahata, who's well-known to all of us in the field, was then led out in handcuffs. The old man was almost in tears as he explained the disease and its dreadful potential. He informed us that he had perfected a vaccine—he could immunize against Viryphus. But so far he hadn't been successful in his attempts to develop an antitoxin.''

Bolan broke in. ''Let's put that in layman's terms and make sure I've got it straight. There *is* a vaccine. So if you're immunized before being exposed to Viryphus, you're safe. But there's no cure if you're exposed before being vaccinated.''

The doctor nodded. ''Precisely. And as you might guess, Takahata had already been forced to immunize Musashi and the rest of his terrorist organization. The doctor stated that he'd been working on the cure when he was abducted.'' Von Studnitz's pipe went out and he paused to relight it. When smoke rose from the bowl once more, he went on. ''When Takahata finished speaking, Musashi returned to the podium with the most shocking news of all. Viryphus had been added to the island's drinking water. We had all secretly received the vaccine in our first meal on the island—all but four of us.'' Von Studnitz took a deep breath. "The madman then read the names of those in the audience who had been exposed to the disease.

"These four men, as well-respected members of the scientific community, will die, Mr. Belasko. They were sacrificed so they could return to the world as proof of Musashi's seriousness."

Bolan stared at von Studnitz. "They're dead?"

"No, no. The disease has a seventy-two-hour incubation period before becoming active or communicable. The four victims had ample time to return to their countries with the news, as was Musashi's plan. But they'll have to be quarantined in—" he glanced at his watch "—fourteen more hours."

A soft knock broke the silence in the living room. A moment later a tall man with a mustache stepped into the room, Bolan's blood-splattered sport coat and ragged slacks hanging from his body.

The President looked up. "Dressing casually this evening, Agent Hart?"

Blood flowed to the agent's face. He glanced at Bolan, then to his gray suit coat, hanging on the chair behind the Executioner. "Excuse me, Mr. President," he said. "I can explain—"

"Don't bother, Greg. I can surmise. Go check the grounds and make sure the rest of your team is accounted for." He paused. "And make sure they're all dressed, will you?" The President coughed lightly. "Later on tonight we'll all have a little talk concerning security."

"Yes, sir." Hart paused for a moment to glare at Bolan, then made a quick about-face and was gone.

The President turned back to Bolan. "To summarize, Striker, Musashi's demands are simple—the release within seven days of seventeen of his Red Army compatriots, currently serving life sentences in prisons of various countries for crimes ranging from trafficking to heroin to brutal, cold-blooded murder. Or the viral-typhus disease will be released."

Bolan frowned. "How does he plan to do this?"

Von Studnitz looked him square in the eye. "According to Musashi, they have a number of viral storage bases set up around the world. Once it's released anywhere, it's only a matter of time before it spreads to each continent. The very air we breathe can act as a conduit, Mr. Belasko. Anyone who hasn't been inoculated with the vaccine will be doomed."

"Can't you reproduce the vaccine?" Bolan asked.

Von Studnitz sighed. "If we knew what it consisted of, yes. Of course. But without Takahata's input, it will take time to discover. And in time will come a cure. But neither will be discovered in the next seven days."

"What are the chances that the JRA's bluffing?" Bolan asked.

Brognola broke in. "None, Striker. That was my first question, too. Tell him, Doctor."

"The blood of the four men who were exposed has tested positive for foreign bodies—both viral and bacterial," he said slowly.

Bolan looked at him. "How long do they have?"

The doctor sighed. "Assuming humans respond to the disease as Takahata's laboratory animals have, they'll die in a matter of hours after the incubation period. But those hours will seem like years. We assume the symptoms will be a combination of typhus and pneumonia. Nerve disorders, red inflammation of the skin and severe respiratory complications, to name only a few."

Bolan addressed the President. "So, I assume that while Doctor von Studnitz and the other scientists work on the cure, you'd like someone to attack the problem from the other end."

The Man nodded. "There's no time for conventional action. We can't negotiate, and we've got one week—seven days. You've got to get to Musashi before he destroys the world."

"Any idea where he is?"

The President shook his head. "We've got very little intel. Nothing on Musashi himself. He seems to have risen through the ranks unnoticed by our intelligence operatives."

Brognola leaned forward, resting his elbows on his knees. "We do know one thing, Striker. The CIA had a low-level snitch within the JRA. At least until recently. Before being discovered and executed, he passed word back to the Company that something 'heavy' was supposed to be happening at different JRA strong sites around the world. But besides his own base in Japan, which has since been abandoned, the only other location he was aware of was somewhere in Sitges, Spain."

Bolan frowned. "Just south of Barcelona?"

"Right."

The phone rang as the President started to speak. He leaned forward and lifted the receiver. "Yes?"

Bolan watched as the President listened, frowning intently at the floor. Then, covering the mouthpiece with his hand, he turned toward the men. "Hot line call," he said. "They're rerouting it from Washington." He turned back to the phone. A moment later he said, "Yes, Mikhail?"

The President listened quietly, his eyebrows dropping to the bridge of his nose. He spoke occasionally, a "yes" or "no." Finally he said, "I'll get back to you soon," and replaced the receiver.

The President moved his head, indicating the phone. "Gorbachev," he said unnecessarily. "The Soviets were aware of our CIA informant."

Bolan saw Brognola's face tighten. "How the hell did he know about that?"

The President waved a hand in front of his face. "It bears looking into, but not right now. The important thing is that he's aware we know the location of one of the storage bases. And *they* have a KGB major who can identify Musashi."

Bolan nodded. "That's not surprising. Until recently the KGB was the JRA's chief source of funds and weapons."

"Yes," the President agreed. "He's proposing a joint operation. They're sending—"

"Look, Mr. President," Bolan interrupted, "I've got no doubt that the Soviet president's intentions are good." He glanced at Brognola. "But the Soviet Union is a nation in turmoil right now. Not every member of the Politburo—let alone the KGB—supports his efforts at reform. Tell him thanks for the offer, but I'll go it alone."

A tired smile crossed the President's face. "I can understand your reluctance. Especially in light of your last encounter with the KGB. But we're all trying to let bygones be bygones these days, and a joint op by the United States and the Soviet Union could mean a giant step for our relationship in the future."

"If Musashi's successful, there won't be a future," the Executioner said bluntly.

The President nodded. "Exactly. Which means we have little to lose. Our intelligence information is almost zero, and seven days is a very, very short time. We can use all the help we can get."

"I won't argue," Bolan said. "But have you considered the consequences if Viryphus falls into the wrong hands within the KGB? The KGB wouldn't try to destroy the world. But they could make far more efficient use of this weapon than the JRA ever dreamed of."

The President exhaled a deep breath. "Yes, that's always a possibility. But it's a calculated risk I feel we've got to take. And we'll have to count on you to see that the disease doesn't fall into their hands once it's located." The President looked him square in the eye. "I wouldn't order you to work with the Soviets, even if I could. But I'm asking. We don't have time for conventional action. Will you take the assignment?"

Bolan frowned. He had nothing against the people of the USSR—they were no different than people the world over. But the KGB—that was a different story. It wasn't, as many Americans naively believed, simply a counterpart to their own CIA. The KGB was a body of secret police and spies that functioned almost independently of the government with very little supervision or control. That lack of control provided the opportunity for numerous factions to breed within the agency. While some of the agents supported Gorbachev's new reforms, others saw them as the road to eventual destruction of the Communist Bloc.

Bolan stared back at the President. On the other hand, the Man was right. They had only seven days, and some risks would have to be taken. The Executioner would have to use any resource available to beat the deadline.

Bolan nodded. "All right, sir. Under the circumstances I don't see that we have any choice."

The four men rose to their feet. The President smiled. "I'd hoped that would be your answer. I'm flying to New York to address the U.N. Security Committee. The Russian agent should be arriving at JFK in—" he glanced at his watch "—a little over three hours. You can ride with me in the helicopter, and I'll send Agents Hart and Cwayna with you to meet the plane and escort you both to Grifiss AFB." He paused, then continued. "I've already taken the liberty of putting a B-1 Strategic Reconnaissance Bomber at your disposal."

Bolan chuckled. "You must have been fairly sure I'd accept the job, Mr. President."

"You've never let this country down, and on this one I was fairly certain."

As they left the cabin and walked toward the waiting helicopter, Brognola reached into the side pocket of his coat, producing a small spiral notebook. "Grimaldi will be with the plane."

"Good." Bolan had no idea where he'd end up in the next few days, and the Stony Man pilot could fly anything from a kite to the space shuttle.

"What other equipment will you need? We'll put it together in Europe and have it waiting for you when you arrive."

Bolan frowned. "I'll have a list for you by the time we hit New York. Try to arrange the pickup as close to Sitges as you can."

Brognola nodded and returned the notebook to his pocket.

"I can notify Spanish authorities if you'd like," the President said. "They might be of some assistance."

Bolan shook his head as they climbed into the presidential chopper. "There's already one leak. And they're more likely to slow things down. But you might stand by in case we need a quick clearance somewhere down the line."

The President nodded. "I'll have your own special mission hot line installed. I'll monitor it myself whenever possible. In any case, I won't be far away. Anything else?"

Bolan nodded. "One more thing. This Russian agent, what can you tell me about him?"

A flicker of humor played at the corners of the President's mouth as the helicopter left the ground. "Quite a bit. Major Platinov is about five foot eight. Computer and electronic expert. Former Olympic-level athlete. And like all KGB agents, I'm sure the major is a competent fighter and marksman. Or maybe we should say marks*person*." He paused, the grin widening. "Platinov is a woman. She'll be wearing a red dress when you pick her up."

THE FLIGHT ATTENDANT pushed the cart down the aisle, gathering plastic cocktail glasses and dinner trays from the passengers on Aeroflot flight number 1726.

Major Marynka Platinov handed the woman her empty dishes, keeping the glass of vodka. She held it to her lips, then set it, still untouched, in the circular cutout of the folding table.

In a matter of minutes now they would land in America, and she'd set foot for the first time in the country. And not just in America, but in New York City. The home of her grandfather.

Platinov smiled, thinking briefly of the stories her grandmother had told her of her American ancestor, Robert Smith. She chuckled softly to herself as her lips silently formed the name. Robert Smith. Names didn't get more American than that.

The KGB officer had never met the man who had come to Russia and given his life in the Revolution. She'd never even seen a photograph of him. But over the years she'd formed a vague image of a shockingly handsome man with strong beliefs.

Platinov's face flushed slightly as she realized that image hadn't crystallized into clarity until after she'd seen an American movie in England. *Reds*. The film had starred the American actor Warren Beatty, and from that time on it had been Beatty that she saw in her mind when she thought of her grandfather.

The attendant walked the aisle once more, stopping to remind negligent passengers that it was time to fold their tables into the seats in front of them. Platinov lifted her glass from the well and handed it to the woman before complying. She sat back in her seat, wondering briefly what America would really be like.

Even a few short years ago, when she was being prepared to compete in the Olympics in Los Angeles, the propaganda machine had still been in effect. All of the athletes, male and female, had been warned not to venture out of their dormitories without their Soviet guides. America was a violent hotbed of crime, they'd been told. A place ripe for revolution, where the minorities were in constant conflict with the repressive government.

Then, in retaliation for the American boycott four years earlier, the Politburo had elected not to participate in the Olympics. Platinov felt a pang of regret flow through her. The chance to see the real America—and a potential gold medal in the hundred-meter dash—had been suddenly stripped from her.

Platinov's mind returned to the meeting with the leader of the Soviet Union only hours earlier. He had been direct. The future of the world was at stake. It might very well depend upon her full cooperation with the Americans. Platinov shook her head. A few short years ago such a statement from *any* leader of her country would have been incomprehensible.

The overhead light flashed in her eyes, and Platinov reached for her seat belt. She pictured her president again, sitting on the other side of the massive desk in his office at the Kremlin. He was a good man, of that she was sure. He was doing everything within his power to free the people of the Soviet Union and at the same time keep the government from self-destructing. The question wasn't his intentions.

The question was his ability. Could he do it? Was anyone capable of such a feat?

Platinov tightened the belt around her waist and ran her hands over her thighs, smoothing her skirt. Her superior, Colonel Rostipovitch, didn't think so. "A weak sister," she'd heard Rostipovitch call the president. The "Jimmy Carter" of the Soviet Union. Although the two men had been friends for thirty years, the colonel firmly believed the president would be the downfall of their country.

The KGB agent took a deep breath. Her country hadn't been so politically divided since the days of her grandfather. Half the members of the Politburo, it seemed, were ready to end the cold war for good.

The other half never would be.

Platinov heard the landing gear drop, and through the window she could see the green waters and islands that made up New York City. Her mind drifted from politics as a twitch of excitement fluttered in her lower abdomen.

She was about to see the birthplace of her grandfather.

Marynka Platinov felt the wheels touch down, and the big airplane taxied to a halt. Gathering her carryon from the overhead compartment, she made her way around the other passengers and up the long jet bridge to the gate.

Two men in gray pin-striped suits stood just beyond the door of the bridge. Platinov studied the suits as she neared the exit. Expensive. The same type worn by the Politburo members. Suits that no amount of saving, or waiting in line, would ever be attainable by the average Soviet citizen.

A big man in a brown leather bomber jacket stood next to the two men. As she stepped through the door to the waiting area, he turned to face her. A rush of adrenaline washed over her as their eyes met, and without knowing why she knew beyond doubt that this was the American agent she would be working with.

One of the men, his eyes hidden behind black plastic sunglasses, wore a neatly trimmed mustache. He nodded to her as she stepped off the ramp. Platinov had heard her leader describe both her, and the clothes she would be wearing, to the President. He in turn would have told these men.

Platinov hadn't planned on going to America when she'd dressed that morning. But the two-piece tailored suit she'd chosen was ironically appropriate for her visit. Regardless of how she might feel about the possibility of a new comradeship between her country and the United States, her true loyalties could be seen in the color of her clothes.

She smiled at the men. Bright red. It seemed a nice touch.

The taller of the two men in the suits stepped forward and extended his hand. "Major Platinov?" he asked.

Platinov took his hand and nodded, trying to see his eyes behind the dark lenses.

His mouth twisted into a forced smile. "I'm Greg Hart, U.S. Secret Service," he said. He turned to his partner. "This is Morris Cwayna." The other man, bald with only a fringe of graying hair over his ears, reached out a hand, which she took. She saw the man in the brown leather jacket from the corner of her eye and involuntarily turned toward him.

Platinov looked up into his eyes. The man's very bearing suggested strength and competence. He was a fighter. There was no mistaking it.

"And this is Mike Belasko," the tall man in the sunglasses added, using Bolan's cover name.

Platinov took his hand, fighting against the strange, tingling sensation the contact sent through her body. She stared into the eyes. Hard. Tough. Yet somehow a little bit sad at the same time. The KGB major held his stare for a moment, wondering briefly if the interest she thought she saw in his eyes was real or imagined.

"The car's waiting," Bolan said, and turned on his heel.

Marynka Platinov and the two men followed him to the parking garage. The two Secret Service men got into a long American sedan, and Bolan inserted a key into the passenger door of a similar vehicle.

"We can discuss our business while we follow them to the air base," Bolan told her, indicating the two men in the other vehicle. He opened the door and reached in, flipping the switch to unlock the driver's side. Leaving the door half-open, he circled the car.

Platinov nodded. Good. He was being polite, but not condescending.

The major took the passenger seat as Bolan started the engine. She glanced at him, feeling the intense physical attraction wash over her again. Yet a moment later she could almost hear the voice of Colonel Rostipovitch, as clearly as if he had been with them in the car. *Your heart must never stand in your way, Marynka. You must retain every advantage.*

Yes, the colonel was right. When the time came, it would be difficult enough to kill this one, as it was.

Bolan guided the automobile around the sharp turns, down seven ramps to the ticket booth on the ground floor. Stopping at the gate, he handed his ticket and a ten-dollar bill through the window, took the change from the outstretched hand and waited for the gate to rise.

The Executioner had been a little surprised that the Secret Service was assisting in this operation rather than the CIA. The President himself had once directed the Company, and Bolan would have guessed he'd have turned to them during such a crisis.

But since taking office, it would have been his day-to-day bodyguards that the Man would feel most comfortable trusting. Times—and loyalties—changed.

Working with the Secret Service simplified things, as well. Greg Hart and Morris Cwayna were already involved, and had what scant intel the Company could provide on the storage base in Sitges. The CIA would have to be called in eventually—the Secret Service wouldn't have the overseas contacts that would be needed. But until then the fewer agencies that became involved, the fewer chances they took that the leak would expand.

The striped arm in front of them rose, and Bolan drove through to the gate. He stopped at the curb, waiting as the Secret Service men behind him badged their way through the ticket booth. Hart nodded from the passenger's seat as they passed, and Bolan pulled in behind them.

As they left the airport proper and turned onto an isolate gravel road, Bolan studied the Russian woman. Her features were sharp, distinct, with the high cheekbones of a Slav. Her eyes betrayed a mixture of heredity, perhaps even a trace of Polynesian or Oriental blood. She was tall and in good physical condition if the muscular calves beneath the dress were any indication.

Wanting to quickly ascertain her abilities, the Executioner had watched her from the corner of his eye as they'd walked from the gate to the car. She moved smoothly, confirming the President's statement that she'd been an athlete.

Bolan's eyes fell once to the shapely calves. He felt his abdominal muscles tighten involuntarily. He couldn't deny the spark he'd felt flash between them when they'd met. It happened from time to time. Sometimes the chemistry between a man and a woman was just there.

As he watched, Platinov dug through her purse, producing an unopened package of Lucky Strikes. She turned to face him in the seat. "All my life I've heard of the quality of the American cigarette." She smiled. "I don't smoke, but I'm curious to try them. You think I'm crazy?"

Bolan caught himself returning the smile. "Maybe," he said. "It's a little early to tell."

Her eyebrows rose, then lowered. "You're making a joke?"

"Yes."

The Russian agent nodded, her face deadpan. She leaned toward the dashboard, depressed the lighter and sat back, waiting. When the lighter popped out, she held it to the end of a cigarette, then looked suddenly at Bolan. "It will bother you? The smoke?"

Bolan shook his head. He turned his eyes back to the road. Okay, he was only human. He'd have to accept the physical attraction this woman inspired in him. But how he handled those feelings was what was important. And any alliance with Marynka Platinov that went beyond that of professionals working together could do nothing but slow down the mission.

And the people of the world didn't have the time to wait. They had seven days.

Bolan turned to the woman. "There are a few things we should discuss. One of them is the fact that I may work differently than you're accustomed to. My methods are effective. We're on a tight schedule, to say the least, and we won't have time to argue about each decision that has to be made along the way." He saw the woman stiffen slightly. What the hell? Now was as good a time as any to get all his cards on the table. "Usually I work alone," he continued, "and I can't say that I'm thrilled about this situation."

Platinov turned sideways to face him. "If you worry because I'm a woman, then—"

"That has nothing to do with it, Major," Bolan interrupted. "It's your intentions that puzzle me."

Platinov's eyes widened slightly. "Mr. Belasko," she said, her face turning red, "my intentions—"

The Executioner shook his head. "Look, don't get me wrong—I not only appreciate, but applaud some of the new directions your president has taken, but quite frankly, the KGB itself has never been number one on my hit parade. I wasn't born yesterday, and I know that not everyone in your government, especially within your branch of it, supports all the changes. And to be honest, right now I'm wondering exactly where you stand."

A new coldness emanated from Platinov's eyes. "I could explain these things to you, but you wouldn't automatically believe me. Still, you would wonder if I lied."

"Probably."

"Then we'll have to take things as they come."

Neither Bolan nor Platinov spoke as they followed the other car onto a blacktop leading to the runway. Hart pulled to a halt. The Executioner parked alongside, stepped from the vehicle and lifted his carryon.

Fifty yards away was a waiting helicopter. Bolan started toward it, the Secret Service men close behind.

Jack Grimaldi, his features shadowed by the bill of an Alaskan bush pilot's cap, stepped forward to meet them. "Ready to roll, Sarge."

Bolan nodded. He turned to the two Secret Service men as Grimaldi loaded the luggage onto the helicopter. Reaching into the flap pocket of his jacket, the

Executioner pulled out a folded sheet of paper. "This is the list of weapons and other equipment I'll need," he said, handing it to Hart. "I'd like to get it in Sitges, if possible, to save time."

Hart took the paper. "No problem."

Bolan stared into the sunglasses. Overpowering Hart and taking his clothes had been unfortunate but unavoidable. He'd made this man look bad—very bad—in front of the President. But since Hart's initial dirty look, the Secret Service man had given no indication that he was holding a grudge. Apparently he was professional enough to realize they had no time for personal vendettas.

Bolan heard the helicopter engine start and the props overhead began to whirl, sending the hair of all three men flying with the turbulence.

Instinctively ducking lower, Hart pocketed the list. "I'll get this to the Company," he shouted above the noise. He shoved a business card into the Executioner's hand. "The name of your contact's written on the back."

The warrior glanced at the card. The picture of a hotel lobby had been printed on the face. Flipping it over, he read the name—Jaime Lopez.

"Lopez will meet you at the hotel," Hart shouted.

Bolan nodded again and turned toward the helicopter. Through the open door he could see Grimaldi at the controls. Directly behind him sat Marynka Platinov, her hands busy with something on the floor between the seats.

The Executioner climbed on board as the KGB major hurriedly closed the top of his carryon.

Bolan stopped at the door. What was she doing in *his* bag? It contained nothing but a few basic items and some survival food. "Looking for something, Major?"

Platinov's head shot up, and she smiled weakly. Staring into his eyes, she said, "I was hungry. We didn't eat on the plane." She held up one of the granola bars. "Do you mind?"

Bolan stared back at her. "Be my guest."

The KGB agent unwrapped the bar and began to eat.

The Executioner took his seat next to Grimaldi as the chopper lifted off the ground. Russian airlines were different than American ones. They didn't always provide food.

Bolan glanced at Platinov as the Russian woman took another bite. Her story about hunger wasn't hard to buy.

Not unless you'd seen the face that went with the story.

THE SUN ROSE in their faces as the B-1B soared over the northeast coast of Spain. Jack Grimaldi, Vietnam vet and reformed Mafia flyer turned Stony Man pilot, dipped the wing and circled over the Mediterranean, back toward the Barcelona airport. As land reappeared in the distance, Grimaldi reduced the power to the turbofan engines and lowered the nose to begin his descent.

Bolan sat back in his seat and watched the runway come into view. While they were in the air, special arrangements for landing the American bomber at the civilian airport had been made through the U.S. air base near Madrid. Bolan didn't know what story had been given Spanish officials as to the reason for the unusual request, and he didn't care. Not as long as it got them quickly through customs with the least amount of exposure.

The Executioner hadn't forgotten the attack by the JRA on Backbone Mountain. There was a leak in the operation somewhere, and he didn't have time to run it down. He had to assume that leak was still operative.

As the B-1B taxied toward the hangar, Bolan turned to Platinov. The Soviet agent had ridden quietly for most of the flight. She, like Bolan, had napped as much as possible in preparation for what they both knew would be a gruelling seven days.

"We go where from here, Belasko?" she now asked, breaking her silence.

Bolan reached into his pocket and handed her the card.

"Hotel Blaumer," she read. "Calle Bonaire, 19-21. Full and half *pensión*. Ocean view." She flipped the card over and frowned. "The name...Jaime Lopez. He's our contact?"

"Yes."

"He's a CIA agent, yes?"

"I doubt if he's an agent, but he's connected to them somehow," Bolan said. "I'm sure you know how things work."

Platinov nodded. "Yes, I'm aware of the routine."

A lone Spanish military officer, medals and leather sparkling, walked toward the B-1B.

Bolan dropped from the plane to the ground and faced him.

"Buenos días," the uniformed man said.

"Buenos días," Bolan replied.

The officer switched to English. "You are Mr. Belasko, I assume?" Without waiting for an answer he continued. "I have instructions to see you and your party through with no delay. I will need only your passport to validate your identities."

Bolan reached into the front billow pocket of his jacket and handed the man his passport. The officer pulled a pair of glasses from the breast pocket of his tunic before opening the document. Then he looked up at the plane as Grimaldi stepped down, followed by Platinov.

The shapely KGB major's red skirt rode high over her thighs as she lowered herself to the ground. Nylon rustled against the garment as she pushed the skirt back down, smiling at the man. With obvious effort the Spaniard returned his eyes to Bolan's passport.

Grimaldi handed over his papers while Platinov rummaged through her purse. The Spanish officer glanced at both documents, briefly comparing Grimaldi's picture with his face before studying the Russian woman closely.

He handed the passports back. "You are free to go," he said, his eyes taking a last inventory of Platinov.

As the man walked back to the terminal, Bolan turned to Grimaldi. "Stick close while we're gone, Jack," he said. "This is only the first lap of the race.

As soon as I know where we go from here, I want to be airborne.''

Grimaldi nodded.

Bolan flagged a cab outside the terminal and opened the door for Platinov before sliding in after her. ''Sitges,'' he told the driver.

The waves of the northern Mediterranean slapped against the beaches, their whitecaps rising and falling as the sun continued to rise in the sky. As they neared the tiny village of Garraf, the highway moved closer to the water, and an isolated resort hotel sprang up along the cliffs.

Bolan watched Platinov from the corner of his eye. The Soviet major was trying hard not to look impressed. But the soft lighting of early day gave the mixture of white sands and rugged cliffs a quixotic, almost surreal atmosphere, and occasionally, when a particularly spectacular view popped up, the woman's eyes widened involuntarily.

Rounding a long, easy curve, they came abreast of the resort hotel. The beaches on each side of the structure glistened like snow under the sun, and Platinov turned to him in awe. ''It is beautiful, yes?''

Bolan nodded, and the KGB major turned her eyes back to the cliffs ahead with unrestrained enthusiasm. Bolan studied her. He didn't begrudge her the girlish excitement. Travel outside the Soviet Union, even for relatively high-ranking KGB officials, was a recent privilege. He just hoped the enthusiasm didn't get in the way of her judgment or performance when the time for action arrived.

As they neared the outskirts of the city, Bolan leaned forward, giving the driver the address of the Hotel Blaumer. Leaning back against the seat, he reviewed what he knew about Sitges. Just south of Barcelona, the town prospered during the summer vacation months, catering primarily to Germans, Dutch and Scandinavians, seeking the relatively lower prices of northern Spain and an ocean closer than the Spanish south.

But people from all over the world could be found in Sitges, and a few Japanese carrying cameras and bullfight souvenirs wouldn't seem out of place.

A few minutes later the driver pulled down a narrow street between tall shops and businesses. Bolan got out, hoisting his carryon, and waited while Platinov grabbed her bag.

A small bar was situated to the left of the lobby. Several men and women, both tourists and locals, sat at the tables, drinking coffee and "eye-openers" of sherry, brandy or the local wine. The tourists talked excitedly among themselves in the electrified voices of travelers anticipating the adventure of another day in a strange land. The locals' eyes were glued to a television mounted on the wall overhead, where the videotape of a bullfight was showing.

Bolan crossed to the desk. A short, stocky man with slick black hair rose from a chair behind the barrier.

"Two rooms, please," the Executioner requested, placing his passport on the desk.

The desk clerk opened the passport, then said, "I am sorry, *señor*. Only one room is available."

Platinov stepped forward, placing her passport next to Bolan's. "One room will do."

The desk clerk's eyes dropped from her face to her breasts, and he grinned at Bolan before turning to pull a key attached to a large ring from the wall. Handing Bolan the key, he said, "I keep *pasaporte* while you are here. You pick it up each time you go out. *¿Entiende?*"

"I understand," Bolan said, and turned to the stairs.

The room had a double bed and a bath with a shower. A small balcony, barely wide enough to hold its two plastic chairs, overlooked the street. Bolan pushed open the double doors and squeezed through, dropping into one of the chairs. Leaning forward over the rail, he looked to his left. A block down the street, between the storefronts at the corner, he could see a small patch of blue sea. He smiled, thinking of the Blaumer's card. So this was the ocean view.

Platinov joined him, taking the balcony's other chair. "We wait?" she asked.

"We wait." The words had barely left his mouth when the knock came.

Bolan had one hand on the Beretta under his jacket as he opened the door. A gaunt man, barely five feet tall, stood in the hall. His ferret eyes darted past the Executioner to Platinov. The Russian woman still stood on the balcony, her hand out of sight in her purse. Looking back to Bolan, he said, "My name is Jaime Lopez."

The Executioner nodded. "Let's go."

He and Platinov followed Lopez down the stairs and into the lobby. Bolan stopped briefly at the desk, pocketing his passport and handing Platinov hers before stepping out onto the street.

The tiny man led them on a winding path, his eyes darting nervously back and forth as they rounded each corner. People of all nationalities crowded the streets, laughing, taking photographs and making purchases. They passed countless street stands selling leather jackets, jewelry and caged birds before turning down a narrow alley.

It was almost noon when they cut through the tables of a sidewalk café to the bar behind. Bolan glanced through the large picture window next to the door. Carefully painted letters on the glass announced the Cantina Cincos Anillos. Lopez opened the glass door and motioned them toward a table.

A waiter arrived and all three ordered coffee. Bolan saw Lopez look nervously toward the rear of the bar. A curtain hung at the end of the long, narrow room. "I'll go check," the Spaniard announced.

The waiter returned with the coffee as Lopez disappeared through the curtain. Platinov raised her cup to her lips, then leaned toward Bolan. "I don't like this," she whispered. "And I don't mean the coffee."

The Executioner nodded. "Something's wrong. Dead wrong."

"He's too nervous."

"It's not his nerves that bother me," Bolan said. "I can accept a case of the rattles. That's an occupational hazard—part of being a CIA snitch. But this place." He shook his head. "Something not quite right."

Just then an American couple in their mid-twenties walked in and took seats at the bar. The man pointed back toward the display window. *"Pulpo, por favor,"* he said.

The woman with him laughed feebly, pointing her index finger at her open mouth in a retching gesture. The bartender cut a tentacle from the octopus, chopped it into tiny circles, placed it on a plate and set it in front of the man.

"That's what I mean," Bolan said. "This place. There are too many people. Tourists. The kind of people who are watching, interested in everything that goes on around them. It's a risky place to pick up a weapons cache. I know what equipment I ordered, and we aren't going to carry it out of here hidden under our jackets."

An Oriental couple dressed in jeans and T-shirts entered the bar. Walking to the table next to Bolan and Platinov, the man set his camera case on a chair, out of sight under the table. Bolan listened as the two spoke quietly—in Korean.

Glancing at his watch, the Korean man rose and walked to the bar. He waited as the bartender set a plate of green beans and potatoes in front of the American woman. Looking back to the woman at the table, he glanced once more at his watch, shook his head and mumbled under his breath.

The bartender turned his back and reached into the refrigerator for two bottles of beer. Still muttering to himself, the Korean strode angrily back to the table, took the woman by the arm and walked hurriedly out the door.

Bolan watched the two cross behind the reversed letters of the Cincos Anillos. He glanced at the empty table. The camera case still sat on the chair.

"He's forgotten his camera," Platinov said.

Outside the window Bolan saw the Oriental couple glance back through the window. They hurried across the street, their eyes still glued to the cantina.

The Executioner sprang from his chair toward the camera case. Platinov looked up, a startled expression on her face.

He dived across the table, grabbed the case by the strap and pulled it from the chair. His eyes flew the length of the room. Twenty, maybe thirty people, men, women and children, sat at the bar and tables. Outside, tourists and shoppers crowded the street.

"What are you—"

"Never mind," Bolan shouted. "Get down!" He sprinted toward the curtain at the rear of the room.

Two men, hats hiding their eyes, stepped from behind the curtain as he neared. The first man pulled a sawed-off double-barreled 12-gauge from behind his back and started to level it at the Executioner's chest.

Screams erupted around the bar as Bolan drew the Beretta. A 3-round burst of 9 mm slugs drilled through the shotgunner's throat. The man jerked spasmodically, his hat falling to the floor to reveal the almond-shaped eyes.

The second gunner reached beneath his leather jacket, grasping the grips of an Intratec Tec-9 pistol. He pushed forward, struggling to swing the weapon out on its sling, the exposed 36-round magazine snagging in the jacket's lining.

Bolan squeezed the trigger, another burst stitching the man chest to face. Behind him, over the screams and shrieks of the bar patrons, he heard the front door open. A gunshot exploded behind him and the glass door of the china cabinet next to the curtain shattered, sending glass shrapnel flying throughout the room.

Bolan turned toward the gunfire. A third Oriental burst through the door, a large-framed revolver in his hand.

The warrior heard a dull click and turned to see Marynka Platinov's hand jerk with the recoil of a Heckler & Koch P7 K3. The German "squeeze-cocker's" first round burned through the wheel-gunner's chest, spinning him sideways. Platinov's wrist jumped again, and another round bored into his temple, driving the man to his side on the floor.

Bolan turned back to the curtain. Ripping it open, he found an unoccupied storage room. Cases of wine, beer and spirits rose from floor to ceiling against the walls. He wondered briefly about Lopez, then saw the half-open door that led to the alley. Darting across the room, Bolan set the camera case gently in the corner, then sprinted back to the bar's entrance.

The Executioner holstered the Beretta and wrapped both arms around the ten-foot china cabinet next to the door. Razor-edged sections of glass fell to the floor, shattering at his feet. He rocked the heavy cupboard, struggling to move it over the door to the storage room. Behind him he heard Platinov sprinting to assist. China and silverware rattled inside as he took a final breath and thrust the cabinet forward over the opening.

A split second later the bomb erupted, the concussion throwing both Bolan and the cabinet backward onto the floor.

The Executioner rolled from under the heavy wood. Platinov came to a halt at his side. "You are all right?" she asked.

Bolan didn't have time to answer. More gunfire shattered the glass door and windows as five JRA terrorists, Uzis and MAC-10s blazing in their hands, burst through the falling glass to send automatic fire sailing toward the rear of the bar. Bolan fired the Beretta dry, downing two of the men, then rolled behind the china cabinet and rammed home a fresh clip. He saw Platinov duck through the door to the storage room, her feet crunching on the broken glass of the bottles, before she leaned back through to drop another gunner.

Bolan rolled from behind the cabinet, firing a 3-round burst into the chest of the fourth gunman. The bolt of the remaining terrorist's weapon locked open as the man to his side fell under Bolan's attack. He looked up in terror, recognition of his own mortality finally registering as his friend's blood flew over his shirt. Screaming, he dived back through the shattered glass of the door and took off down the street.

Bolan scrambled to his feet. "Let's go," he shouted to Platinov, and raced for the front of the bar.

THE HAUNTING RUMBLE of the *taiko* drum called the contestants to the workout room. Ichiro Musashi opened the flaps at the rear of his face mask, positioned the chin rest and pushed it back against his forehead. Snaking his arms through the *kote* guards, he stepped from the mat to the polished hardwood floor.

Another man, similarly dressed in the armor of kendo, took his place at the center of the room. Musashi watched Toshi's hands, which shook slightly. Face hidden by the canvas-covered metal, the leader of the Japanese Red Army smirked at the man.

Good. Toshi seemed even more nervous than usual.

Toshi Senzaki was by far the best sparring partner Musashi had within the Japanese Red Army. He easily defeated all those who challenged him.

All, except Musashi. Musashi's smirk widened into a grin. Toshi had one vital weakness, a character flaw that had not only prevented him from ever defeating the JRA leader, but had kept him from scoring a single, solitary point during the countless times the two squared off against each other.

Toshi's technique was impeccable, his movements sharp, evasive, deceptive. He was quick, and possessed seemingly limitless endurance. No, Musashi thought, as the referee stepped between them to extend his flag. Toshi's disadvantage came in no way from his physical ability as a swordsman.

Musashi watched the bamboo sword quiver in the man's hands. His opponent's problem was mental. He was aware of Ichiro Musashi's samurai heritage—of the famous ancestor who had spawned the lineage that would finally produce the greatest warrior the world had ever seen. And because of that knowledge, Toshi didn't *believe* he could defeat Musashi.

For that reason he never would.

"*Rei!*" The referee's voice was hoarse and gravelly. Musashi bowed to the man who faced him, then stepped forward into the *maai* position, bringing the bamboo *shinai* up, on guard. The JRA leader felt his muscles relax as he prepared for battle. He smiled again beneath the mask. Relaxation was the reason he had called for the kendo session. Even the descendant of the greatest master strategist in history needed recreation from time to time, something to relieve the stress that accompanied his destiny.

His plan was progressing relatively well. It had been ever since he'd ferreted out the CIA informant and sliced off his head in front of the others, letting the traitor's death serve as fair warning to anyone else who might consider similar treachery.

But a few things hadn't gone as smoothly as he would have wished. The American agent was still alive, the ambush on the mountainside having failed miserably. He had now teamed with Marynka Platinov, the KGB agent who'd once supplied the JRA with money and guns.

The situation would soon heat up. But now, before it reached the boiling frenzy that he knew was to come, before the time arrived when he would need all of his wits rested, all of his faculties sharp, he would relax and rest his mind.

"*Hajime!*" the referee brought his flag down.

Without hesitation Musashi leaped forward. Raising the bamboo sword overhead, he brought it down in a swift, fluid movement, scoring with a strike to the left side of his opponent's mask. Toshi staggered backward.

The referee's hand shot upward. *"Men ari!"* he shouted, announcing the point to the head. He extended his flag toward Musashi.

Musashi and Toshi resumed their positions in the center of the ring. The referee signaled, and Musashi began a slow, circling movement to his right. He watched as Toshi mirrored his movements, the tip of his sword shaking with his nervousness.

At the dojo door Musashi saw Junko and Keiko step into the hall. Junko, as always, wore the wrinkled green army fatigues that had become her trademark. A short-bladed knife hung from her belt. Musashi watched Keiko from the corner of his eye. Junko's newest lover couldn't be more than twenty.

Musashi stepped forward to block a sudden slash to his ribs. The follow-up blow struck Musashi squarely between the eyes and sent him sprawling to his back on the wooden floor. His eyes blinked uncontrollably as they struggled to focus on the sparkling lights above. From somewhere far away he heard the referee's surprised voice announce the point. Toshi had scored. Shaking his head, Musashi rose unsteadily to his knees.

The JRA leader felt the referee's hand grasp his canvas jacket and help him to his feet. Shock turned to humiliation.

Knocking the referee's hand roughly to the side, Musashi suddenly realized that Toshi had fooled him. He hadn't been more nervous than usual today. His exaggerated fear, like the preempted cut to the ribs, had been nothing but a feint, setting up the JRA leader for the bold strike to the center of the head.

Musashi ripped off his face mask and cast it to his side. Next came the arm guards, the *do* protecting his chest and the rest of the kendo armor.

Slowly Toshi pulled his mask away. "I'm sorry honorable—"

Musashi held up a hand to silence him. "Don't speak. What you've done is good. So good, in fact, my friend Toshi, that we'll dispense with such protection as befits only the amateur." He turned to the referee. "The match point will be decided with the wooden swords." Turning on his heels, he strode across the floor to the wall.

Musashi glanced down the long row of weapons that hung from the racks. Reaching up, he selected a long wooden sword and thrust it through his belt, then turned back to the center of the room.

The JRA leader started across the mat, then a sudden thought caused him to return to the wall. Grinning, he pulled a shorter weapon from its resting place and slid it into his belt.

Musashi watched as Toshi returned to the center of the room, his own wooden sword held tightly in both hands. This time honest fear and apprehension radiated from the man's sweating face as they took their places.

"Hajime!"

Musashi felt the hatred course through his veins as he drew his weapon and thrust forward in the quick-draw-and-cut style. Toshi stumbled backward, awkwardly blocking the backhand slash to the head. He countered feebly, his sword sweeping toward Musashi's shoulder at half speed.

Transferring the long sword to his right hand, Musashi drew the short sword from his belt with his left. The crack of wood against wood resounded through the open room as he brought it up to stop a halfhearted attack by his opponent. Ducking under the weapon, Musashi whirled in a circle, bringing his long sword around behind him to smash into Toshi's unprotected ribs with a sickening, crushing sound.

Halting his spin, Musashi brought the short sword flashing back in a vicious, whiplike arc. The half-sharpened hardwood blade struck Toshi across the cheek, opening his face from mouth to ear.

Musashi stepped back, both weapons up and ready. Toshi dropped to the floor, his stark white jawbone shining through the crimson that flowed from the gash. Groaning softly, he opened his mouth to spit blood and teeth on the floor. Five feet from the fallen man's side stood the referee, his lower lip drooping in shock and horror.

Musashi laughed out loud. "Match point."

Dropping both weapons onto the floor, he turned and left the dojo.

4

Bolan sprinted down the street after the men, Platinov right behind him. As they neared a pastry cart at the corner, the man in the blood-covered shirt ran headlong into a beggar carrying an armload of cardboard scraps. The scraps flew through the air as the old man grunted and fell against the cart, sending rolls, doughnuts and crepes smashing into the sidewalk.

Both terrorists disappeared around the corner.

Slowing at the corner, Bolan fired a glance at both sides of the street. Nothing. Then, from halfway down the block came a scream. The man in the blood-splattered shirt broke from behind a fruit stand, shouldering an elderly lady to the pavement as he sprinted away. A second later the other JRA gunner bolted across the street and into an alley.

Bolan pointed Platinov across the street, and the Russian woman sprinted for the alley, narrowly missing a Renault as it screeched to a halt in front of her.

The Executioner took off after the blood-covered terrorist, dodging the cursing shopkeeper and scattered fruit the man had left in his wake. Two blocks later Bolan saw the bloody man pull a pistol from under his shirt before he ducked around another corner and out of sight.

Bolan somersaulted to the ground as he reached the corner and hit the concrete with his shoulder before rolling to his feet, two feet under the gunshot he knew would be waiting. Aiming down the street at the gunman, he fired a shot that ricocheted off the edge of a building as the JRA man disappeared from sight once more.

Like a tailback in broken field, the Executioner maneuvered down the street, darting around shocked faces and frozen bodies. He slowed at the corner and peered around the edge.

Two blocks down he saw the white sands of the beach as the man in the bloody shirt raced seaward. Dropping the Beretta's sights on the fleeing man, Bolan sighted down the barrel. He needed the man alive—needed to question him. It was vital that he learn the exact location of the viral storage base in Sitges, and anything the man might know concerning Musashi's base camp.

But he couldn't allow the terrorist to continue running rampant down the streets of the city, firing blindly and risking the lives of countless innocent bystanders.

As the Executioner's finger tightened on the trigger, a young man and woman, both wearing backpacks, stepped out onto the sidewalk. The man, bearded and in faded Levi's, moved directly into his line of fire.

The Executioner eased his grip.

The running terrorist dodged the bearded man and collided with the woman, her long blond hair whipping around her neck as she spun back into the shop. The JRA gunner fell onto his side, rolled to his feet and fired three shots in Bolan's direction. People on the street screamed, dropping to the sidewalk. The gunman fired again, and the slide of the automatic locked open. He threw the empty weapon onto the ground, turned and dashed toward the sea.

Bolan slid the Beretta back under his jacket and took off after the man, closing the gap. He was less than a block behind now. He'd catch him. And the threat to innocents had ended. If the terrorist had held more firepower, he'd have already drawn it.

The man in the blood-splattered shirt hit the beach, turned right and pounded across the sand. Bolan raced after him, sprinting across the beach as the JRA man stumbled over a large woman in a string bikini, knocking her to the ground. The woman sprang to her feet, her breasts swinging freely as her loose top fell to the sand. Raising a fist toward the runner, she slapped her biceps with the other hand and sent a long stream of German profanity after the terrorist. Bolan hurdled the woman's overturned lounge chair and earned his own curses as the topless woman leaped out of the way.

With less than a twenty-yard lead now the JRA terrorist cut suddenly from the beach and away from the ocean. Bolan turned back with him, angling to cut him off when he reached the street.

As the Executioner's foot hit the concrete, a horse-drawn cart carrying bottled water rounded the corner, separating him from his prey. Diving to the side, he avoided the cart and saw the terrorist disappear down another alley.

Bolan heard the first of the sirens, now several blocks away. He rolled to his feet and sprinted toward the alley. Somewhere to the north he heard a gunshot, followed quickly by three more rapid-fire pistol rounds.

Rounding the corner, the Executioner saw the JRA gunman slow his pace, ten feet away from where the alley dead-ended in a brick building. Bolan drew the Beretta and shouted, "Freeze."

The JRA gunner ground to a halt in front of a steel door. More sirens joined the rising pandemonium in the distance as he slowly turned to face the Executioner, his fearful face becoming a fierce mask of hatred. "You cannot stop us," he said through gritted teeth. "And I will tell you nothing."

Bolan started toward him, the Beretta leveled on his chest. "We'll see."

Suddenly the steel door swung open and a young Spanish woman stepped into the alley, her arms filled with plastic bags. She looked from the terrorist to Bolan, then froze in her tracks, a short scream choking itself off in her throat.

The JRA man leaped to her side, encircling one arm around her neck while the other drew a long dagger from beneath his bloodstained shirt. The woman gasped, her packages falling in a pile around her feet.

Grinning, the terrorist pressed the tip of the knife into her throat.

Bolan raised the Beretta, and the man crouched farther behind the woman.

"Drop the gun," the terrorist screamed, "or she dies."

Bolan watched the man between the rear sights of the 93-R. His head and most of his body were hidden behind the woman. The warrior took a deep breath. The only target he had was the top of the man's shoulder, extended two inches to the side of the woman's tear-streaked cheek.

"Drop it!" the terrorist repeated. "Drop it, and I will let both of you go."

The Executioner felt a snort escape his lips. He held no false hope that that would happen. The moment he let the Beretta fall from his hand, the woman was as good as dead. The screaming madman would punch the knife through her throat.

The woman's fate lay in his hands. She had only one chance of survival, and that chance depended on the Executioner's shooting skill.

Without hesitation Bolan squeezed the trigger, sending a 9 mm hollowpoint echoing down the narrow alley and into the terrorist's shoulder.

A high-pitched squeal rose from the wounded man's throat as the force of the round spun him away from the woman and back into the bricks. The knife fell harmlessly to his feet.

Forgetting the scattered packages, the terrified woman raced past the Executioner and out of the alley.

Bolan ran forward as the terrorist reached down and grasped the handle of the dagger. Gripping it in both hands, he turned the tip toward his abdomen. He looked up as the Executioner neared, his eyes brimming with fire. "I will tell you nothing!" he screamed for the last time.

Bolan left his feet, diving forward through the air, knowing full well he'd be too late.

The JRA gunner drove the knife into his bowels, jerked upward and to the side and fell forward onto his face as the Executioner landed on top of him.

From behind Bolan heard the clatter of heels on the concrete. Looking up from the disemboweled body, he saw Marynka Platinov jog toward him. She came to a halt by his side.

"He's dead?"

Bolan nodded. "Yours?"

"The same."

The warrior rose from the ground. The sirens he'd heard earlier sounded nearer. "We've got to get out of here," he said and, reaching for the steel door into the building, found it unlocked. He jerked it open and ushered Platinov inside.

They found themselves in a short hallway. Through the window in the door at the end of the hall, Bolan could see that they stood, literally, on the doorstep of a shopping mall. They entered the mall next to a record and tape store, walking swiftly past the blaring flamenco music that assaulted them from inside. Bolan led Platinov down the hall to the front. As he reached for the door, a police car pulled to a halt outside.

They turned back in the direction they'd come, passed a tobacco shop and ducked into a small beach-wear boutique.

Bolan directed the KGB agent to the women's side of the shop. "Get a swimsuit and any other gear you'll need at the beach."

The warrior grabbed the first swimsuit in his size and hurried to the dressing room. Undressing quickly, he slipped into the suit. He used the Leatherman's knife blade to sever the price tag before throwing the light safari jacket back over his shoulders. Rolling both the Desert Eagle and Beretta into his slacks, he emerged from the dressing room.

Platinov stood in front of a long row of basket-woven beach bags on the wall. A midthigh-length shift fell from her shoulders, riding high over the back of her legs as she reached up to pull one of the bags from its hook. The Russian woman stuffed her bright red suit inside, then turned to him, holding the mouth of the bag open as he crammed his pants and shoes on top.

A uniformed police officer, walkie-talkie held to his mouth, hurried past the shop as they approached the counter. Quickly selecting two pairs of sunglasses and rubber thongs, they donned both before paying for their purchases. Then Platinov took his arm as they strolled inconspicuously back down the hall, stopping periodically to gaze into the windows at hand-crafted jewelry, mantillas and Talavera porcelain.

As they walked casually toward the front exit, a tall policeman with a handlebar mustache turned toward them, a puzzled frown knitting his brows. Platinov squeezed Bolan's arm. "We must call the children to-night," she said in an irritated tone of voice. "If you don't get drunk again. Your drinking is ruining the whole vacation. You've got to..." She let her voice trail off as the policeman changed course and hurried away.

Bolan waited until a large guided-tour group as-sembled near the front door and nudged Platinov into the middle. Merging with the group, they shuffled through the exit to the bus waiting outside.

Bolan and Platinov passed the bus and crossed the street, cutting quickly around the corner to the beach. They followed the beach to a stand selling American hot dogs and other refreshments, and took a table nearby. Bolan dropped the jacket from his shoulders and walked to the stand, returning a moment later with a pitcher of sangria and two glasses.

He set the pitcher on the metal table as Platinov pulled the shift over her head. Dropping it uncere-moniously to the sand, she sat down across from him. The tiny black bikini bottom disappeared from view as she crossed her legs and poured a glass of sangria.

On the street behind them a police car crept by. Bo-lan saw both officers scanning the beach as they passed. He turned back to Platinov. "What hap-pened on your end?"

Platinov shrugged. "I chased him perhaps a mile, almost to the edge of the town. I was hoping to take him alive in order to question him." She held the glass to her lips, took a sip and grimaced. "It's too sweet," she said, setting it down.

"Go on."

"As he neared a cluster of houses, he suddenly turned and fired. I was forced to kill him."

Bolan watched as she reached into the pitcher, removed a wine-soaked section of orange and placed it between her lips. "Any idea where he was headed?"

Platinov chewed the orange thoughtfully, her eyebrows lowering. "To one of the houses, I think. They were all that remained before the town ended."

"How many houses?" Bolan asked.

"Four. Maybe five." Her eyes fell to his chest, then darted back to meet his. "I didn't have time to count."

The Executioner sat back in his chair, taking a small sip of sangria as another police car cruised by. He raised his forearm, squinting at his watch under the blazing sun.

Time was moving.

Platinov leaned forward across the table, the black bra of her swimsuit opening slightly to reveal the tops of her breasts. Looking over the plastic frame of her sunglasses, she asked, "What do we do now?"

Bolan shook his head. "There's only one course of action at this point. We've got to recon those houses. Determine somehow if that's where the Viryphus supply is being held."

"And if that isn't the place?"

"Then we're back to square one. With less time than before."

Platinov shoved her sunglasses back onto her nose and uncrossed her legs. "When do we go?"

Bolan watched another squad car pass. "As soon as we can."

THE BRIGHT COLORS dulled and smiling faces disappeared as Bolan and Platinov passed from the tourist district into the peasant section of town. The sand of the beach deepened in hue to a wet, dirty brown, and here and there they saw the remnants of old tires, frazzled canvas shoes and rusty bedsprings. Children still played in the incoming tide, but rather than the bold print and iridescent swimsuits sported by their counterparts near the hotels, the peasant children wore the remnants of clothing that had long ago earned its right in the dustbin.

A long row of deteriorating shanties bordered the edge of the town. The Executioner looked up to see five modern houses built into the cliffs in the distance. A narrow car path led from the street by the beach, away from the poverty below and up to the affluency only a half mile away.

"This is the place," Platinov said. "We had come from the other direction." She pointed back up the street. "But it was toward these houses that he ran."

Bolan scanned the terrain ahead. The path leading upward was open. They'd have no cover during the ascent, and anyone watching from the houses would spot them the moment they left the beach.

The Executioner squatted, lifting a handful of moist sand and letting it trickle through his fingers. If this *was* the site of the Sitges Viryphus supply, then the JRA was bound to have surveillance. Particularly in light of what had happened earlier that morning.

The houses might have another approach, another road on the other side. But chances were good that it would be equally exposed to any curious eyes from the cliffs.

A donkey brayed loudly, and Bolan turned to see an old man in a ragged green work shirt and pants lead the animal from a paint-chipped outbuilding next to one of the shanties. Across the scraggly grass in front of another crumbling dwelling, an equally impoverished form dragged a small cart loaded with oranges. Rising from the sand, Bolan led Platinov toward the men as they hitched the donkey to the cart.

Both men looked up as they approached. The man in the green shirt said, *"Buenas tardes."* His three-day growth of gray-and-white whiskers danced into a smile. *"¿Naranjas?"* he asked through rotten teeth as he pointed at the oranges.

"Yes," Bolan answered in Spanish. "Many oranges." He dug through the straw bag to his pant pocket, peeled a large bill from the roll and extended it.

The gray-whiskered man's eyes opened wide. "I don't have change for that."

"I don't want change," Bolan replied. "I want them all. And the cart." He waved his hand over the oranges. Reaching back into the bag, he produced several more bills. "And the donkey," he added, indicating the animal.

The old man's phlegmy eyes opened wider in shock as he took the money.

"And I want to buy your clothes." He turned to the other man. "Yours, too."

Bolan and Platinov followed the old men into one of the shacks. Cockroaches scampered across the floor and broken furniture as they entered, then went about their business, unmindful of the human intrusion as both men stripped to long underwear.

The Executioner stuffed his jacket into the bag and took the tattered green shirt from the old man, slipping his arms through the sleeves. Eight inches of chest held the buttons from their holes, and he let the garment drape from his shoulders. The frayed trousers hit him midcalf as he pulled them on over the swimsuit.

Platinov lifted the shift over her head, oblivious to the old men's leers as her black string bikini came into view. She slid into the other man's brown trousers, then started at the tail of his soiled chambray shirt, buttoning it to the throat.

The gray-whiskered man stared at her breasts as they disappeared under the shirt. Turning to Bolan, he spoke rapidly in Spanish.

"What did he say?" Platinov asked as she tucked her hair under a stained felt hat.

"He wants to know if you're going to try to pass as a man."

The old man's eyes returned to her chest. Shaking his head, he spoke again.

Bolan smiled. "He says that only a fool would fall for it."

Platinov's cheeks colored slightly. Without answering she looked down at her hands, tucked the shirt into her waistband and zipped the pants.

Still in their underwear, the old men followed Bolan and Platinov outside. Pointing in the direction of the cliff houses, the Executioner spoke again in Spanish. He felt a sudden rush of adrenaline as the man with the whiskers answered. Giving each man another large bill, he turned to the orange cart.

Bolan took the donkey's reins and led the animal toward the path, Platinov at his side. Turning his back to the hills, he stuffed both the Desert Eagle and Beretta into his pants and covered them with his shirttail. He filled his pockets with extra magazines as Platinov slipped the H&K and a Soviet Makarov automatic into her waistband.

Bolan glanced at the woman. The baggy clothes helped some, but beneath the threadbare garments the obvious lines of her femininity still showed through. "The old man had a point," he said. "Keep your head down and stay behind me. Don't give them a clear view."

Platinov dropped to the rear of the cart. "What did he say about the houses?"

Bolan spoke in a whisper as they started up the narrow path. "They're all owned by foreigners. German or Dutch, he thinks. He used to try to sell them fruit, but they rarely bought anything. The climb's hard on his knees, so he quit trying."

"Is that all? You looked as if he'd said something more important."

"He did. For the past few months he's seen Chinese going in and out of the second house."

Behind him he heard the KGB agent take a deep breath. "Chinese. That would be an easy enough mistake to make."

Bolan didn't answer. Guiding the cart around a series of rocks, they drew abreast of the first house. He glanced quickly up the road to the next residence, feeling the watching eyes that had to be inside.

The Executioner left the reins in Platinov's hand and walked to the door of the first house. Raising his hand as if to knock, he studied the next house down.

The two-story dwelling faced the cliffs, a concrete staircase leading down to the shore below. The Executioner's eyes moved back to the house. Five feet above ground level, a rough cedar porch ran the length of the front. The back door of the house stood open. The sounds of rock and roll, the lyrics in Japanese, flowed through the screen.

Bolan returned to the cart. "Follow me on up," he whispered to Platinov. "We're selling oranges. As soon as we get to the door, it's on." The Executioner took the reins and led the donkey closer.

They were fifteen feet away when the first shot rang out. Bolan saw the hole appear in the screen as the explosion rocked from the house and reverberated through the cliffs. The bullet smashed wetly through the oranges in the cart.

From inside the house Bolan heard the scream. *"Amerikajin!"*

A fusillade of automatic rifle fire enveloped Bolan and Platinov as they dived to the ground.

ROUGH HANDS GRASPED his shoulders, pulling him to his feet. Dr. Toshiro Takahata rubbed the sleep from his eyes as they tried to focus on the two men in front of him.

"Enough sleep!" one of the guards shouted in his ear. "Work!"

Takahata shuffled slowly toward the bathroom as the guards prodded him along with their rifles. Pulling his toothbrush from the rack on the wall, he twisted the hot water knob and leaned over the sink.

Cold water dripped slowly from the tap as the doctor brushed his teeth. He had learned early that it made no difference which of the handles he used—the water would always be cold.

Spitting, Takahata braced both hands on the edge of the sink and pushed himself upright. Sharp pains shot through his lower back. The shower in the small room adjacent to his sleeping quarters was the same. Cold. It did nothing to relieve the torturous burns and needle jabs that raced from his back down his legs with every movement.

The old man replaced his toothbrush and turned wearily toward the guards. He glanced longingly at the mat on the floor as he pulled his ragged cardigan from the nail in the wall.

The bright lights caused him to squint as he left the room and walked down the corridor. Rarely had he gotten more than three hours' sleep since Musashi and the rest of his thugs had kidnapped him from the research outpost, drugging and blindfolding him so that he had no idea where he went. First, it had been the deceitful mockery of the research seminar that they had sponsored, drawing his fellow colleagues from all over the world in his name.

Then to this place. Takahata glanced at the ceiling, dripping with moisture, as they walked down the hall. They were underground. Of that he was almost certain.

But where underground he couldn't imagine.

One of the guards opened the door to the laboratory while the other shoved him through. Takahata took a seat at his desk and opened his notebook, staring bleary-eyed at the page. He glanced quickly at the armed men standing at the door, then returned his eyes to the desk.

Musashi seemed to have no understanding that an exhausted man couldn't function. Perhaps it was his age. Still in his early thirties, his own youthful strength hadn't yet begun to fade. The megalomaniac seemed intent on working him to death—first, supervising the manufacture of enough Viryphus vaccine to inoculate his entire organization of hoodlums, now, in a breakneck attempt to find an antitoxin for the deadly disease.

A total, all-encompassing blackness invaded Toshiro Takahata's soul. *He* had created this terror that might well destroy the earth. *He* was the one with whom the responsibility ultimately must rest.

Leaning forward, he folded his arms on the desk and buried his face in his hands. From the corner of his eye he saw the letter opener.

Takahata's hand moved slowly toward the foot-long piece of steel, then stopped. The letter opener wasn't sharp enough. Using it, he would never be successful in an attempt to save face by performing seppuku.

The old man took a deep breath. And ritual suicide would be the coward's path, at this point. There was still a chance, however slim, that someone, somewhere, would destroy Musashi before his plan went into effect. Or more likely, considering the time element, Musashi might be defeated after the Viryphus strain had been let loose on the world. If that were the case, a ready and available antitoxin would be vital.

And he was the only man in the world who had the knowledge to discover that cure in time.

Takahata felt a hand grasp his hair and jerk his head upright. A hand slapped him across the back of his neck, knocking his glasses to the floor. "Work!" the familiar voice commanded.

Looking at the floor, Takahata saw that the earpiece had broken from the frames of his glasses. He reached for the pieces, feeling his back suddenly catch. Grimacing, he pushed both hands against his knees and straightened.

"Work!"

Without speaking the old man reached across the desk, tearing a strip of clear plastic tape from the dispenser. He wrapped the tape around the earpiece, securing it to the frame, then pushed the spectacles onto his nose. They jutted oddly from his face as he returned his eyes to the notebook.

Mocking him on the page, he saw the list of his attempts to find an antitoxin. A line had been drawn through each, crossing it out. Each new bacteriophage he exposed to the mutant disease had retained the capacity for multiplication, seeming to thrive on the infected cells rather than neutralize them.

Takahata closed the notebook. He had reached for a microscope on the desk when the laboratory door flew open. The old man swiveled in his chair to face the door as Ichiro Musashi strutted in. He felt a thick, bilelike revulsion in his throat as the man walked toward him. Musashi was dressed in a long, flowing kimono, a matching, three-piece set of swords thrust through his belt. He stopped halfway to the doctor, turned back toward the open door and snapped his fingers.

Junko Tamano entered the room. Takahata stared at her, and she returned the stare, her eyes showing no remorse, no sorrow for her treachery.

Musashi strode to his desk and stopped. Callous, brutal eyes met the doctor's. "Your work is progressing?"

Takahata looked wearily up at him. "Slowly."

Musashi's eyes narrowed. "Then you must increase your pace, Doctor. Time is of the essence."

The old man felt his weariness and fear turn suddenly to rage. In his selfless attempt to rid the world of typhus, he had made an innocent mistake. He looked at Junko. He had been betrayed, then forced to assist in this madman's plot to rule the world.

The old man's face hardened. "I don't understand your impatience. All members of your group have been vaccinated. You're safe from the disease. Since you're intent on destroying the world, what need do you have of a cure for Viryphus?"

"It's not your place to question my motives, old man," he said. "But since you've had the courage to ask—a courage I hadn't seen in you before—I'll tell you." He leaned forward, his face less than an inch from Takahata's. "I'm not a fool. I realize that many nations will foolishly resist my invitation to surrender. When they don't meet the deadline, I'll be forced to set your creation free. With the realization that m⁻

threat has become reality, the world will be in chaos. The antitoxin will give me further bargaining power.''

He paused, studying the doctor's face. ''Besides, old man, I don't wish to destroy the world. Each life I take is a life that could have served me. If the world population ceases to exist except for my own people—'' he waved his hand around the room, indicating Junko and the guards ''—then I'll have accomplished little. I already rule these people.'' Musashi threw back his head and laughed hysterically.

Takahata felt his anger peak. ''No!'' he screamed. ''I won't aid you in this insanity!''

The movement was a blur in the old man's weary eyes. A moment later he saw Musashi wipe the blade of the long sword on his kimono and return it to the scabbard.

Takahata looked at where his hands rested on the desktop. The tip of his left little finger rocked briefly back and forth, then settled in a growing pool of blood.

The old man raised his hand. Transfixed, he watched the blood pulsate from the wound just below the nail. Dropping his hand, Toshiro Takahata fell to the floor, the bile in his throat turning to vomit pouring from his mouth.

Musashi dropped to a squatting position next to him. Grabbing a handful of hair, he turned the doctor's face to his. ''You *will* assist, old man,'' he said softly. ''Or you'll die the death of a thousand screams.''

''My... finger...'' the old man moaned.

Musashi walked to one of the cabinets along the wall and opened a drawer. Pulling out a metal first-aid kit, he turned and threw it at the prostrate man. "You're a doctor," he said. "Sew it up."

Takahata watched Ichiro Musashi and Junko leave the lab, then slowly hauled himself to his feet.

"Sew it up!" one of the guards commanded. "Then, work!"

Takahata nodded.

5

More shots rained down from the second story as Bolan and Platinov sought cover. Coming out of a shoulder roll, the warrior sprang to his feet against the wall next to the door, the Desert Eagle filling his hand. To his rear the KGB major yanked the Heckler & Koch from under her waistband and took cover behind an outcropping of rocks.

The Executioner caught Platinov's eye and pointed to the side of the house. The KGB agent nodded and sent a steady stream of covering fire ripping through the screen while he crab-walked to the corner.

Moving cautiously around the side of the house, Bolan ducked under a window and raised his head to peer over the edge. Two JRA terrorists, both armed with Kalashnikov assault rifles, stood in the center of the rear bedroom, their weapons bucking in their hands as they fired excitedly through the door.

The Executioner triggered a .44 Magnum round from the Desert Eagle into the chest of the closer man, then dropped below the sill as return fire transformed the window into thousands of tiny slivers that rained down over his head. Staying close to the ground, he moved toward the cliff side of the house.

As the corner of the rough cedar porch came into view, Bolan heard a door open and feet pound across the porch toward him. A short, stocky Oriental wearing a "Rising Sun" headband leaped from the porch, an AK-47 gripped in both hands. He twisted to face Bolan as he fell through the air.

Stark horror covered the falling man's face as a .44 Magnum round drilled into his chest in midair. The limp form jackknifed and fell to the ground, crumbling into a heap at Bolan's feet.

Hurdling the body, the Executioner pulled himself onto the porch and pressed his back to the wall. A large picture window separated him from the door. Risking a quick glimpse through the window, he saw a man holding a shotgun. The barrel of the weapon fluttered in the man's hands as he jerked it back and forth, nervously covering the window.

Retracing his steps, the Executioner dropped back to the ground. The distinctive sound of the assault rifles continued to boom from the back of the house. They were answered periodically by the crisp crack of Platinov's pistol.

Bolan hoisted the body with the headband to the porch. He held the man upright, then shoved him past the picture window. The dead arms flailed in the air as two blasts of 12-gauge shot took out the window, then diced through the body as it hit the porch.

Bolan stepped in front of the window and fired three quick shots into the room. The shotgunner fell forward onto the carpet as the Executioner stepped through the broken glass and into the house. Ripping a fresh magazine from his back pocket, he shoved it into the Eagle while he scanned the room.

A small kitchen was to his left, and to his right a narrow staircase curled upward through a large round entrance to the second floor. Against the far wall a hall extended perpendicular from the living room. From the door Bolan heard the muffled din from the ongoing battle between Platinov and the gunman in the back bedroom.

He paused briefly, evaluating the situation. His eyes darted to the staircase. The rounds being fired from the second story sounded as if they came from a single gunman. But if he moved upward at this point, the man from the back room might suddenly decide to retreat to high ground.

The Executioner would find himself in a cross fire.

And unless she could somehow get away from the rocks, Platinov could do little but defend her position. He'd be unable to depend on her to keep either JRA gunner occupied.

No, Bolan realized as he crossed the room to the hall, he had to neutralize the gunman at the rear of the house before moving upstairs.

Bolan scanned the hall, seeing an L-shaped turn just past an open door. He moved to the door, peering around the corner into an empty bedroom. The clamor of rapid fire mounted as he made his way quietly down the hall, dropping to his knees and risking a look.

The man he'd shot through the window now lay on the floor in the middle of the room. Kneeling next to the bed, his back to the door, the remaining gunman fired a long burst of automatic rounds through the shreds of screen that remained in the back door.

From the back of the house came the sharp crack of a 9 mm pistol, and the kneeling gunman's head snapped back as if he'd been hit in the forehead with a baseball bat.

A new volley of rounds erupted from the second floor, then Platinov burst through the door, the H&K gripped in both hands. Looking up, she saw Bolan in the hallway and eased her grip, her weapon clicking loudly as it uncocked in the sudden silence.

Without speaking Bolan raised the Desert Eagle and pointed toward the ceiling. Platinov nodded, and together they made their way back down the hall to the staircase. Platinov started to ascend, but Bolan reached out and grabbed her arm. Shaking his head, he whispered, "Too risky. He had to have seen you come inside."

"Yes," the Russian woman agreed. "He shot at me all the way."

"And by now he's figured out he's alone. He'll be waiting to pick off the first head that pops through the opening."

"What do we do?"

Desert Eagle extended overhead, Bolan moved under the staircase. "Can you hear me?" he shouted up through the opening.

There was a long pause, then a vaguely familiar voice said, "Yes."

The Executioner frowned. Where had he heard that voice? Suddenly it dawned on him. "Lopez?" he asked.

A long pause was followed by "Yes."

"Well, Jaime, I wondered what had become of you. Listen closely. I'm going to run the situation down to you. If you miss anything, be sure to stop me so I can explain. Your life depends on your understanding every word." He paused, letting it sink in. "All your friends down here are dead. You'll be, too, unless you drop the rifle down the stairs, then follow it. Slowly. Show your hands first and keep them in sight the entire time. Understand?"

A short laugh came from above. "I don't need to follow your instructions, Belasko," the man replied. "You can't climb the steps without exposing yourself."

"That's true," Bolan conceded. "Which is why I just plan on lobbing a few grenades upstairs if you don't start down in the next thirty seconds."

Bolan waited. The man upstairs remained silent. Finally the Executioner called, "Fifteen seconds."

The unseen voice trembled slightly as it said, "You lie. You have no hand grenades."

"Ten seconds."

"Let me see the grenades if you have them."

"Sure thing," Bolan said. "Stick your head through the opening. I'll show you. Five seconds."

An AK-47 bounced down the stairs. A moment later a set of hands extended hesitantly over the side.

"Come on," Bolan prodded. "We're waiting."

Slowly, his empty hands held high, Lopez descended the stairs, his eyes darting from Bolan to Platinov as his lips quivered uncontrollably.

When he reached the bottom, Platinov stepped forward, running her hands around his belt, then up and down his legs. "He's unarmed," she announced.

Bolan directed Lopez to the couch and shoved him to a sitting position. "Playing both sides of the fence, are you, Jaime?"

Lopez didn't answer; Bolan hadn't expected him to.

The Spaniard's eyes leaped furiously around the room, then fell on Bolan. "You don't have grenades. I knew it."

Platinov snorted. "If you did and came down, anyway, then you're even more stupid than I thought."

Bolan tapped the Desert Eagle lightly against Lopez's forehead. "I'll make this short and sweet. You're going to take me to Musashi."

At the sound of the name the man's head jerked upward.

"But first," Bolan went on, "I want the supply of Viryphus that's stored here."

"There is none."

Platinov leaned forward. "As the Americans are fond of saying, bullshit." She slapped the man across the face.

"As you can see," Bolan said, "my Russian friend doesn't share either my good nature or my patience. Now, I'll ask you once more—"

"It's the truth," Lopez pleaded.

Platinov unbuttoned her cuffs and began rolling up the sleeves of her shirt. "It seems we are in for a long evening, Belasko. But not as long for us as it will be for him."

Terror shot through the eyes of the man on the couch. "You must believe me. I'm no hero. The Viryphus was transferred earlier this afternoon... after we received word that the attack at the cantina had failed."

"Where?" Bolan asked.

"I don't know."

Platinov sighed wearily, then crossed the room to the kitchen. The fear in Lopez's eyes grew as he heard the Russian woman rummaging through drawers.

"What is she searching for?"

Bolan shrugged. "With her you never know."

Platinov returned, carrying a box of matches, a cheese grater and a large pair of pinking shears. Kneeling at the Spaniard's feet, she began to cut a zigzag pattern up his pant leg to his crotch. The Russian woman looked up into the startled man's eyes. "Did you like women?"

"What?" Lopez looked nervously at Bolan, then back. "Of course. I *do* like women. Why do you ask?"

"I like to become acquainted with those I must interrogate," Platinov said as she started on the other pant leg. When she reached the top, she cut sideways across the placket, then ripped the ragged garment from the man's bony legs. "Do you sing, Jaime?" she asked calmly.

"What? Why do you ask such a thing?"

Platinov shrugged. "I'm just curious. I was wondering if you were a soprano... before. Never mind. It doesn't matter." She reached for the cheese grater.

The horrified man looked at Bolan once more, his frightened eyes pleading. The Executioner raised both hands, palm up, and shrugged.

Platinov opened the box and struck a match. She held it to the cheese grater. The metal began turning a dingy brown as it heated.

"Wait!" Lopez screamed. "I'm telling you the truth! The supply has been transferred."

"Where?"

"To Pamplona."

Platinov put down the cheese grater and blew out the match. "*Where* in Pamplona," she demanded.

"I don't know."

Platinov sighed again and reached for the box of matches.

"No!" Lopez roared, tears forming in his eyes. "You must believe me. I don't know!"

"How are they transporting it and how long ago did they leave?" Bolan asked. To his side, he saw Platinov strike a match, then blow it out.

"Two...two and a half hours ago. They're driving a dark blue Toyota van. They planned to stop overnight somewhere, then arrive early in the morning."

Platinov struck another match.

"Please!" Lopez moaned. "I don't know where."

"Where's Musashi's base camp?" Bolan asked.

"Please! You must believe me. I don't know!"

Bolan shoved the Desert Eagle back into his belt and lifted the phone from the end table next to the couch. Dialing the Barcelona airport, he watched the Russian woman casually lighting, then extinguishing matches while he waited for Grimaldi to answer the page. Lopez watched her in horror.

Finally Bolan heard the voice. "Yeah, Sarge."

Bolan gave him directions to the house on the cliff. "Rent a small plane, Jack. No, better yet, make it a chopper. You can set it down on the beach just below us. We'll be waiting for you." Returning the receiver to its cradle, the Executioner turned to Platinov. "I'll make a quick search." He nodded toward Lopez. "Keep the cheese grater handy in case he's lying."

Bolan started upstairs. Working clockwise, it took less than ten minutes to search the second story. An undefinable uneasiness swept over him as he moved from room to room. He couldn't put his finger on it, but something was out of place. He stared at the elaborate Moroccan furniture, the Indian pottery on the shelves, the prints of Spanish art framed on the walls. He shook his head.

Downstairs again, he started in the rear bedroom, working his way around the bodies and toward the front of the house. In the closet of the bedroom that had been empty, he located a false wall behind the shoe rack. Opening it, he found an empty storage space.

Satisfied that he'd uncovered every hiding place large enough to contain the Viryphus supply, he started back down the hall to the living room.

Lopez cowered on the couch as the Executioner reached the end of the hall. The skinny double agent faced away from the door, toward Platinov. Her back to both Bolan and Lopez, the KGB agent had the phone pressed into her ear, whispering in Russian.

As Bolan stepped into the room, Lopez made his move. Springing suddenly forward, he grasped the pinking shears on the floor in front of him.

"Platinov!" Bolan shouted as his hand shot to his belt for the Desert Eagle.

Still holding the phone, the woman pivoted on the balls of her feet. Her left leg rose to her knee, then shot out in a vicious side kick. The knife edge of her bare foot struck the little man in the throat, and he fell to the floor.

Platinov hung up the phone and knelt by Lopez's side. "He's dead."

"Who were you talking to?" Bolan demanded.

The woman looked up. "My superiors."

"Why?"

The KGB agent's face flushed, then she scowled at him. "That's my business."

Bolan walked forward, gripping her upper arm firmly. "Wrong. When I agreed to work with you, it became *our* business."

Platinov twisted away, fire in her eyes. "This isn't an American mission, Belasko," she said angrily. "It's a joint operation, and I have progress reports I'm expected to make."

"So why did you wait until you thought I was out of earshot?"

The KGB agent didn't answer. Bolan stared back into the enraged eyes and thought briefly of the incident involving his bag on board the helicopter. The woman was holding cards she hadn't yet shown, running some sort of parallel mission that might, or might not, put the race for Musashi and the viral-typhus disease in jeopardy.

From outside the house, Bolan heard the sound of rotors. Stepping out onto the porch, he saw the lights of the chopper descend as Grimaldi passed over Sitges.

The Executioner looked away from the lights into the darkening sky. There was no way they'd spot the van from the air after dark, even if they knew where the JRA terrorists planned to stay. Their best bet was to fly directly to Pamplona and hope the JRA didn't arrive before sunrise.

Bolan crossed the front yard and started down the steps leading to the beach. Hearing feet on the concrete stairs behind him, he turned and looked over his shoulder. Platinov had changed back into the bright red suit and was following him down to the beach.

The Executioner turned to face the helicopter as Grimaldi set it down on the sand, knowing it wouldn't be the last time he checked his back.

THE HELICOPTER shuddered in the heavy wind as it hovered over the Pamplona city limits. Bolan pressed the eyepiece of the Bausch & Lomb Discoverer against his eye, using the wide fifteen-power field of view to scan bumper-to-bumper traffic heading into the city below. To his right, Platinov did the same with her binoculars.

A dark rectangular shape topped the hill just before the city and slowed as it encountered the long line of vehicles. The Executioner rolled a finger across the power control ring, zooming closer.

"You can see it?" Platinov asked.

"Yeah. A van, all right. Dark blue. But it's a Chevy." Bolan returned the lens to the wider angle and resumed searching the traffic.

The flight the night before had been uneventful. Grimaldi had set the chopper down just off the highway and stood watch while Bolan and Platinov had grabbed a few hours of much-needed sleep. The Stony Man pilot had awakened them both just before daybreak, pulling the whirlybird skyward once more as the sun had brought on new visibility and with it new hope.

Platinov let her binoculars drop to the end of the strap and turned to Bolan. Bright red blotches marked the spots above her eyes where the eyepieces had pressed into her forehead—visible proof of the stress and strain of the mission. The woman rubbed her eyes. "They're all beginning to look the same, the cars. Is this city always so busy?"

Bolan shook his head. "It's festival time."

"Festival?"

"The Feria de San Fermín," the Executioner answered. "Bullfights. Drinking and dancing in the streets."

"Ah, yes. I've read of it. Ernest Hemingway. The bulls chase the men through the streets, yes?"

"Yes." Bolan watched another dark van top the hill. He rolled the Discoverer to the 60 mm objective lens, seeing the outlines of a Toyota. "Take her down again, Jack."

For what seemed like the thousandth time, Grimaldi dropped the helicopter through the air, swooping down a few hundred feet above the highway.

Bracing the Discoverer on his knees, Bolan strained through the eyepiece as the van crept slowly through the traffic. As he focused the scope, a laughing Latino face behind the wheel began to clarify. The man raised a wineskin to his lips and squeezed the sides, squirting a stream of red liquid into his mouth before passing the container to an outstretched hand behind him.

Grimaldi took the chopper back up.

Bolan watched through the scope as another van neared the long line of cars. Ordering Grimaldi lower, he waited. A moment later he discerned a grim face, and a Rising Sun headband tied around a man's forehead.

Next to the driver sat the man who'd left the camera bomb in the Cantina Cincos Anillos.

"Bingo," Platinov said. The KGB agent dropped the binoculars from her eyes.

"Take her back up before they spot us, Jack," Bolan directed. "Let's see where they go."

The helicopter moved high above the long stream of traffic as the van crossed into Pamplona. Bolan watched through the spotter's scope. As they neared the center of town, with its twisting streets and boisterous revelers, it became increasingly more difficult to follow the tiny blue speck.

The Executioner pressed the scope closer as the blue dot below turned a corner. "Take her down, Jack," he said. "If we don't do it now, we'll lose them."

Grimaldi nodded. "Sure would be simpler just to drop a few grenades, Striker."

Bolan shook his head. "Even if we had them, we'd risk blowing up the Viryphus and lots of innocent people. And if the disease got loose in this wind, we'd have done Musashi's work for him.''

Grimaldi shrugged as the chopper lost altitude. ''Just wishful thinking.''

''What *are* you going to do?'' Platinov asked.

Grimaldi grinned behind the sunglasses. ''You'll see.''

Bolan slid the Discoverer into the case as the chopper dropped through the air. He waited until Grimaldi brought them to a halt, hovering fifty feet in the air just behind the van. Below, the line of cars passed between the storefronts on each side of the street. Several heads looked up from the throng of pedestrians that intermingled with the traffic.

Inching open the door to his side, the Executioner squeezed through the opening. The fierce, hot winds from the chopper blades beat down on the warrior's head as his feet found the landing rail. Carefully sliding his hands down the steel supports, he squatted on the thin strip of metal while Grimaldi dipped lower.

Screams of delight drifted upward as the celebrators watched the chopper descend. From somewhere close by came the brassy sounds of bullfight music. The Executioner looked toward the front of the line. Two blocks ahead, toward the center of town, a police officer halted the traffic. A second later a uniformed marching band began crossing the intersection.

The crowd broke out in applause as the helicopter drew near, clapping and laughing at the unexpected bonus to the festivities. Through the window in the back of the van Bolan saw another almond-eyed face. Then a rifle barrel appeared through the glass as Grimaldi guided him carefully forward and over the vehicle.

Bolan released his grip, spreading his arms and legs to drop the last ten feet through the air. A roar of acclaim went up from the crowd as he landed facedown on the van.

The Executioner hit the thin metal, denting it slightly, as he came to rest on the roof. Almost simultaneously he heard a muffled explosion inside the van and a gray-edged hole appeared in the roof to his right.

He rolled away from the hole, his fingers fighting to find purchase on the luggage rack as two more holes appeared in the roof. The van swerved from the street and jumped the curb.

The Executioner held on as the Toyota passed the cars ahead, frightened pedestrians scurrying to the side as it made its way along the sidewalk. Instinctively he rolled across the roof, his legs swinging over the side as a duet of rifle shots sounded and another pair of holes appeared where he'd lain.

Bolan's legs scraped against the bricks of the buildings as the Toyota swerved away and back to the street, angling toward the marching band and the astonished policeman. The sound of trumpets and trombones suddenly ceased as the musicians dropped their instruments and scattered for cover. The officer's hand shot for the flap on his holster as they raced past and through the oncoming traffic.

The van's right front tire hit an abandoned tuba, the soft brass smashing and fastening itself to the wheel. The van skimmed across the pavement, then reversed directions and skidded out of control as the driver overcompensated.

The Executioner saw it coming, and there was nothing he could do.

Jumping the curb on the other side of the street, the Toyota sailed across the sidewalk and into the plate-glass window of a jewelry store. The vehicle fishtailed through the display room, overturning counters and sending salesmen and customers scurrying out of its path.

Bolan held on as glass and metal rained over him before the van struck the back wall of the showroom. The concussion threw him forward over the hood and into the wall as the Toyota rebounded a few feet backward. He slid down the wall in front of the van, his head spinning from the collision. He looked up to see the man in the headband grin evilly through the windshield, then reach for the stick on the steering wheel.

Bolan dived to the side as the Toyota's engine roared. He hit the ground a split second before the van barreled into the wall once more.

Screams of delight came from the sidewalk as fes-tival patrons charged through the open front to dig furiously through the sparkling gold and diamonds in the rubble. The delight turned to horror as the driver leaned out the window and fired four rounds from an automatic pistol.

Bolan rolled to his feet while the looters hit the floor. He drew the Beretta as the driver threw the van in reverse, the tires squealing back across the tile. Holding the weapon in a two-handed Weaver's grip, the warrior pumped two rounds through the side window and into the man's brain.

The van slowed but continued toward the sidewalk. Bolan fired another round, which shattered the windshield. A follow-up shot took out the man riding shotgun as the van stalled, half in, half out, of the jewelry store.

The van's back door popped open as Bolan raced forward, hurdling the terrified bodies on the floor. He was halfway across the shattered glass of the display counters when the side door slid open. Two men jumped from the back onto the sidewalk, and one of them, wearing a cutoff black sweatshirt, reached back and grabbed a small cardboard box from the floor of the van.

The vehicle's side door rolled open and two gunners appeared, both holding Uzis and opening up with a steady stream of full-auto gunfire. Bolan hit the floor, razorlike shards of glass slicing through his skin as he rolled through the debris. He fired two 3-round bursts into the van, tracking first into one gunman, then the other.

The Executioner sprang to his feet and sprinted to the sidewalk. He heard the helicopter overhead as Grimaldi and Platinov hovered high in the air. Scanning the street, he saw the JRA men spring toward the center of town. Holding the Beretta at his side, Bolan gave chase.

A half block ahead, he spotted the terrorists dodging their way through the merrymakers. Carrying the cardboard box under his arm like a football, the man in the cutoff sweatshirt stiff-armed his way through a party of street dancers. His partner shouldered past a man tipping a straw-covered wine bottle to his lips. The wine drinker spun to the ground, cursing.

Bolan sprinted on. Wooden barricades closed off a street ahead, and on the other side of the wood hundreds of men wearing white shirts with red scarves tied around their necks looked nervously behind them.

The two terrorists reached the barricade and turned to face him. Then, turning back, they vaulted over the side.

From several blocks to Bolan's left came the loud, hissing sound of a fireworks rocket soaring skyward. A moment later he heard the explosion as the rocket burst into tiny pieces.

The mass of men in white begun running, pushing and shoving as they screamed in delight. The terrorists disappeared into their midst.

Bolan reached the barrier and leaped over, his feet hitting the ground as a second rocket exploded. Running as best he could, he spotted the man in the head-band fifty feet to his left. The warrior pushed forward, fighting to make his way to the terrorist, the running crowd blocking his path. Then, from behind, he heard more screams and the thunder of running hooves against the cobblestone pavement.

Looking briefly over his shoulder, he saw several men dive for cover in doorways as the lead bull raced past them. The tip of a horn caught the shirt of one man, puncturing the material and trapping him. With a mighty twist of his neck the bull sent the man flying into the air and through the splintering wood of the barricade.

Bolan leaped to his right as the bull drew beside him, rolling back to his feet as the animal sailed past. He scanned the running mass ahead. The black sweatshirt had disappeared in a sea of white and red.

The clamor of more hooves drummed the stones to his rear. Two more bulls passed to his left, sending one man flat against the nearest wall while another rolled into a fetal position next to him.

Twenty yards ahead the man in the headband darted from in front of a group of runners and leaped up on the barricade as the bulls passed. Looking behind him, his eyes widened as he saw Bolan nearing.

The JRA man dropped from the barricade as Bolan heard more bulls behind him. He turned to see four of the snorting animals running shoulder to shoulder. Glancing quickly around, he saw the doorways filled to overflowing and men in white and red hanging neck to neck from the barrier.

The Executioner stopped in his tracks, turning to face the oncoming bulls. The animals raced toward him like a battery of artillery tanks.

Bolan centered himself in the street. Waiting until the middle bull was ten feet away, he raced forward between the outstretched horns and grasped the back of the animal's burly neck. Instinctively the beast raised its head, catching the Executioner just above the belt line. With a mighty jerk the bull sent him high into the air and behind the charging horde.

Bolan hit the ground on his side, scrambling against the barricade as another bull trampled over the spot where he'd fallen. Rising to his feet, he raced on.

Far ahead he saw the first of the runners reach the bullring and burst through the gate, the lead bulls close behind. With room to maneuver now the white-clad runners turned to face the enraged animals, waving their scarves in mock veronicas and turns.

The two JRA men, running side by side, came into view as they neared the gate. They both jumped for the barricade as the main throng of animals passed and burst into the ring.

From behind, Bolan heard a final bull bearing down. He turned briefly, remembering the second rocket that had gone up. It signified that one bull had fallen behind the pack and should be watched for after the others had passed. The Executioner moved out of the way as the bull, head lowered, raced ahead.

The JRA men were ten feet from the ring when a dozen white-clad runners converged on the gate. Screaming in terror as the last bull closed in on them, they blocked the narrow opening as they fought to crowd through.

Both terrorists turned toward the bull as it charged. Stark fear filled their eyes as they realized they had nowhere to run. Then, the man with the box reached out with his free hand, wrapping his arm around the waist of his comrade. Bending his knees slightly, he lifted the startled man and turned him toward the bull like a shield.

The hulking brute's right horn vanished into the chest of the man in the headband, then reappeared through his back, dripping blood. The force of the assault broke the grip of the man with the box, sending him sprawling back into the swarm of bodies at the gate. Two of the white-clad runners caught him by the arms and pulled him through the opening to the safety of the bullring.

The wounded man's mouth opened wide, and a shrill shriek escaped his lips. Then the sound ended abruptly as a river of crimson gushed out. The bull raised his horns, shaking the terrorist in the air like a rag doll. Then the mammoth animal thrust him over the rail into the crowd and walked calmly through the gate.

Bolan rushed past the bull and saw the man with the box racing toward the far side of the ring. As he reached the wall, he sent the box overhead, then pulled himself up and into the stands.

The Executioner sprinted across the ring, dodging bulls and men. As he reached the wall, he saw the man in the sweatshirt disappear down a ramp beneath the bleachers. The warrior vaulted the fence and raced down the winding ramp to the street. The whirl of Grimaldi's blades overhead met his ears as he scrutinized the area.

Nothing. The man with the box was gone.

From high overhead the Executioner heard Grimaldi's voice on the chopper's PA system. "A block left, Striker! Then cut right!"

He increased his pace, forcing his own discomfort and pain from his mind. The rapid blasts of firecrackers assaulted him from all sides as the people celebrated the first running of the bulls and the opening of the festival.

As Bolan closed the gap, the man with the box turned, drawing a small automatic from his belt. He fired three quick rounds, the blasts blending into the explosions around them. The warrior fell forward to the pavement, the bullets sailing harmlessly over his head. Turning again, the man with the box ran to the front door of a one-story house.

The Executioner drew the Beretta and leaped onto the porch as the man entered the house. Lowering his shoulder, he exploded through the door.

A round of 12-gauge buckshot hit the wall next to him, two of the shot slicing through his shirt as the man with the box took cover behind a couch. More gunfire sailed past from the side as the warrior fired across the living room to a hallway, dropping the Japanese with the shotgun.

The man in the sweatshirt raised his head from behind the couch. Bolan fired a quick round that drove him back to hiding. Turning to his side, the warrior tapped three 9 mm hollowpoints into the dining room and saw a terrorist with a wispy mustache fall to the floor. The AK-47 in his hands fired wildly as it jammed open and fell from his grip. Lamps fell from the end tables and clay pottery on the shelves exploded under the assault of the unrestrained rounds.

A gasp came from behind the couch as the AK fired itself dry. Bolan turned back to see the man in the sweatshirt fall from cover, a single, blood-spurting hole just above his left eyebrow. The cardboard box flew through the air, hit the floor and rolled to a stop in the middle of a pile of shattered pottery.

Footsteps sounded on the porch behind him, and Bolan turned in time to see Platinov burst through the door, the H&K held upright in a two-handed grip.

A sudden burst of fire assaulted them from the kitchen, and two more terrorists stepped into the room. The Executioner dropped one with a round between the eyes while a double-tap from Platinov's squeeze-cocker sent the second man tumbling to the floor.

The house suddenly quieted. Quickly Bolan did a room-to-room search. Shoving the 93-R back into the shoulder rig, he returned to the living room.

Platinov stood facing the door, the H&K covering the opening. Bolan beckoned, and she turned to follow him to the box in the corner.

He brushed the broken pieces of earthenware aside with his foot. Dropping to his knees, he reached forward and set the box upright. A bullet hole, the edges brown and scorched, stared back at them from the cardboard.

Platinov let out a gasp. "Is it the..." Her voice trailed off.

Bolan didn't answer. He opened the box and withdrew a long metal cylinder. The soft steel bent concavely where the bullet had entered. Turning the cylinder around, he saw the jagged flanges formed by the bullet's exit. A dark green mossy substance covered the side of the tube where the vacuum created by the round had brought some of the contents with it.

He looked into the cardboard box. The same mossy substance dripped down the sides of the empty container.

The Executioner set the box back down amid the broken pottery and turned to Marynka Platinov.

Neither spoke.

DOUBLE YOUR ACTION PLAY...

"ROLL A DOUBLE!"

Peel off label & place inside

CLAIM UP TO 4 BOOKS
PLUS A DYNAMITE BONUS GIFT
ABSOLUTELY FREE!

SEE INSIDE..

NO RISK, NO OBLIGATION TO BUY...NOW OR EVER!

GUARANTEED

PLAY "ROLL A DOUBLE" AND GET AS MANY AS FIVE GIFTS!

HERE'S HOW TO PLAY:

1. Peel off label from front cover. Place it in space provided at right. With a coin, carefully scratch off the silver dice. Depending upon what is revealed beneath the scratch-off area you are eligible to receive up to 4 books PLUS a bonus gift ABSOLUTELY FREE!

2. You'll receive ''hot-off-the-press'' Gold Eagle books never before published. Send back this card, and we'll rush you the books and gift you may qualify for.

3. And afterward, unless you tell us otherwise, we'll send you 4 action-packed books every other month to preview. They're guaranteed to be the best of today's action adventure fiction. If you decide to keep them, you'll pay only $12.80 for each shipment—that's 15% off the cover price for all four books! And there's no extra charge for postage and handling!

4. You must be completely satisfied. You may cancel at any time simply by sending us a note or a shipping statement marked ''cancel'' or by returning any shipment to us at our expense.

DETACH AND MAIL CARD TODAY!

"ROLL A DOUBLE!"

PLACE LABEL HERE

SCRATCH HERE

**SEE CLAIM CHART
BELOW**

164 CIM AC7A

YES! I have placed my label from the front cover into the space provided above and scratched off the silver dice. Please rush me the free book(s) and gift that I am entitled to. I understand that I am under no obligation to purchase any books, as explained on the opposite page.

NAME

ADDRESS _____ APT.

CITY   STATE   ZIP CODE

CLAIM CHART

	4 FREE BOOKS PLUS DYNAMITE BONUS GIFT
	3 FREE BOOKS PLUS BONUS GIFT
	2 FREE BOOKS

CLAIM NO. 37-829

GOLD EAGLE NO-BLUFF, "NO RISK" GUARANTEE

- You're not required to buy a single book—ever!
- You must be completely satisfied or you may cancel at any time simply by sending us a note or a shipping statement marked "cancel" or by returning any shipment to us at our cost. Either way, you will receive no more books; you'll have no obligation to buy.
- The free book(s) and gift you claimed on this "Roll A Double" offer remain yours to keep no matter what you decide.

If offer card is missing, please write to:
Gold Eagle Reader Service, 3010 Walden Ave., P.O. Box 1867, Buffalo, N.Y. 14269-1867

DETACH AND MAIL CARD TODAY!

6

KGB Colonel Rotislav Rostipovitch dropped the receiver into its cradle and turned in his swivel chair, his weary eyes staring across the room at the opposite wall.

A brief glow of pride swelled in his chest as he looked at the long line of pictures. Third from the left, on the second row, he saw a slightly younger version of himself wearing a bright red sweat suit. Just in front of him, a little to the left, was the beaming face of a young woman in a track singlet. A gold medal hung around her neck.

Rostipovitch stared into the woman's sultry brown eyes. Those eyes had changed little since the picture had been taken. A few crow's-feet at the corners perhaps, but they seemed to add to the face's strength rather than deter from its beauty.

Pressed between the photo and the glass in the bottom left-hand corner of the frame was a white slip of paper. His eyes were too tired to read the faded ink. He didn't need to. He knew the words by heart.

Moscow Games. 1980. Marynka Platinov. 100-meter dash.

Rostipovitch sighed. Playing the part of a track coach had been a relaxing phase in the life of the career KGB man. It had enabled him to travel the world, to see the other, inferior forms of government that oppressed the masses while catering to the rich. It hadn't bothered him that the people of democracies seemed happier. That happiness was nothing but illusion. Perhaps they *were* more free than their Soviet counterparts, but only for the moment.

The colonel rubbed his eyes. It didn't matter if the people of other countries were more free. The only road to true freedom lay in being part of the social structure. And that could only be achieved completely through communism.

The problems that had plagued the Soviet Union since the Revolution had to be expected. Great social structures weren't built overnight. They didn't come into being in a matter of months or years—not even within the span of one lifetime. But someday, Rostipovitch told himself, someday when the wrinkles had finally been ironed out, the dreams of Marx and Lenin would materialize.

If the Soviets didn't destroy themselves first.

Reluctantly the colonel returned to the two-foot stack of reports that littered his desk. Hungary. Poland. Czechoslovakia. East Germany. Bulgaria. And now Romania—what had happened *there?*

Rostipovitch felt his heart skip a beat. How far behind could Mother Russia herself be? Step by step the greatest power the world had ever known was dissolving.

The fluttering in Rostipovitch's chest intensified. Without thinking, he fished the tiny bottle of nitroglycerin tablets from the side pocket of his coat and dropped one of them under his tongue.

He reached for the folder labeled Bulgaria and opened it before him when the phone buzzed once more. "Yes, Ivanna?"

"Major Platinov is on the line. Do you wish to speak with her?"

Rostipovitch almost screamed. His heart pounded like a jackhammer as disconcertment swept over him. He had given Ivanna clear instructions to give Platinov complete priority—to put her through *immediately* each time she called. It was just this type of incompetence, this inability to follow direct orders, that lay at the root of the Soviet Union's problems.

Controlling his voice as best he could, he replied, "Yes, Ivanna. Put her on."

A moment later Rostipovitch heard a click, and then a series of crackling sounds echoed over the line. Platinov's businesslike yet feminine voice said, "I must speak quickly."

"Go ahead."

"We're in Spain, Colonel," she continued around the scratching. "We've located the storage base in Pamplona."

"And?"

"The Viryphus supply was released but has been sealed off in the house in which it happened." There was a short pause. "Belasko and I have been exposed to the disease."

The colonel's mind raced. "You have *what?*"

"We've been exposed to the disease and have seventy-two hours to complete the mission before we become carriers."

Rostipovitch felt his frustration turn to a hollow, empty despair. He pressed the receiver tighter into his ear and fought to maintain his poise. "Then you must work quickly. Has Belasko been neutralized?"

The colonel heard another long pause, then above the crackling, a softer voice said, "No."

Rostipovitch felt the veins in his temple twitch as his hand tightened around the receiver. With his other hand he lifted a pencil from his desk and tapped it against the open file. "Explain immediately," he ordered.

"It hasn't been necessary."

A mixture of despair and outrage threatened to overwhelm him. His voice rose an octave as he said, "Your orders were to eliminate the American as soon as you had obtained what information he had."

The line crackled and snapped. "My orders are confusing, Colonel. The president instructed me to work with—"

Rostipovitch tapped the pencil against his desk. "He has reevaluated the situation and now agrees with me that the Americans can't be trusted. So, as you can see, Major, your orders are no longer confusing. You must eliminate Belasko immediately."

"But, Colonel, I may need him to help locate—"

Rostipovitch's fingers tightened around the pencil. "Must I remind you that the Soviet Union is in a weakened state? If the Americans come into possession of the viral-bacteria, it will be used against us."

"Colonel, I don't believe that Belasko—"

The pencil in Rostipovitch's hand snapped in two. "You will carry out your orders, Major," he thundered into the phone. "Orders given to you not only by myself, but by the supreme leader of the Soviet Union." The colonel paused, wiping a bead of sweat from his forehead with the back of his hand. "Do you understand?"

Platinov's voice was hesitant. "Yes."

"Have you determined the location of Musashi's base?" Rostipovitch asked.

"Not yet."

"Where do you go next?"

The line popped and crackled in his ear. "We... I'm not certain. Wait. I must go. Belasko's coming."

Rostipovitch heard a click and the line went dead.

The KGB colonel replaced the phone and leaned back against the chair. His eyes returned to the photograph on the wall, and he felt a nausea rise from his stomach to his throat. He had loved Marynka Platinov since the moment he'd laid eyes on her, many years ago when he had masqueraded as one of her coaches.

But even then he'd been an old man—an old man fearful of rejection and perhaps even ridicule at the hands of one so young and beautiful. Rostipovitch sighed. He had never allowed himself to broach the subject.

And now he'd never have the chance.

The dream of an eventual life with Marynka Platinov had gotten him through many cold, lonely nights in his tiny one-room apartment. The odds of turning fantasy to fact had always been remote—but possible. Until now.

Marynka Platinov had contracted the deadly Viryphus disease, and she would die.

Tears clouded his eyes. Wiping away the wetness with his sleeve, he opened the file in front of him. His eyes refused to focus on the paper. Platinov was one of the only two loves he had had in his life. Now he would certainly lose her. And he was in danger of losing the other.

Would Platinov kill Belasko? He had heard the hesitancy in her voice. Why? Was she in love with the American? Sharp pangs of jealousy shot through his chest. It made no difference—not now.

Tremors of despair quivered through his heart, intensifying the arrhythmia. Rotislav Rostipovitch picked up the phone. He knew what he might have to do if he was to save the only love that would remain in his life when Marynka was gone. "Get me the president," he told Ivanna.

While he waited for the connection, Rostipovitch reached into the bottom drawer of his desk and withdrew the bottle of vodka. He held it to his lips, taking two quick swallows, then replaced it. Just a little, he told himself. Just a little to calm the nerves.

He heard the line connect. "Yes, old friend?" came the voice from the Kremlin. "You have heard from the major?"

"Yes, Comrade," Rostipovitch answered. He felt the sweat on his forehead break out again as the vodka warmed his stomach. "She and the American are in Spain. They are nearing the base camp."

"Where is the base camp?"

Rostipovitch hesitated. "I don't know. She was forced to end the conversation just before relaying that information."

"Is she cooperating with the American agent?"

"Yes, but it appears that *he* is a problem. She's certain he intends to obtain the Viryphus for the CIA. I feel it's imperative that I join them immediately." Rostipovitch held his breath.

A long sigh of disgust met his ears. "Colonel Rostipovitch," the Soviet leader said, "we've discussed this point of view many times in the past few days. I have no love for the American CIA, but the immediate threat to the Soviet Union—to the entire planet— is a weapon of cataclysmic proportions in the hands of a madman. It's with *this* problem that we must concentrate our efforts. You will remain here." He sighed again. "In this matter, at least, the concerns of the United States and Soviet Union run parallel."

"But we must look ahead," Rostipovitch protested. "The Americans have proved themselves to be liars. With one breath they preach peace. With the next they invade Panama on the pretext that Noriega is a drug smuggler. They—"

"Yes, yes, Colonel. The same type of things we've done over the years in Czechoslovakia, Hungary and many other countries. We're paying now for those mistakes. The Americans will eventually pay for theirs. And if we don't solve the immediate problem quickly, there will be no 'ahead,' as you say, to look forward to." He paused. "But I don't intend to argue with you. You and Platinov will give the American your full cooperation. Is that understood?"

"Yes, Comrade," Rostipovitch replied. He heard a click.

The phone still gripped in his fist, the KGB colonel leaned back in his chair and stared at the wall. Then, punching the intercom button, he raised the receiver to his ear one final time. "Ivanna," he said, "make arrangements for my plane to be readied for immediate takeoff."

"When will you leave?"

"I don't know yet. Have it ready."

"May I give a destination?"

"You may not."

Rostipovitch retrieved the vodka bottle and downed another long pull. He stood up and walked to the wall. He stared at Marynka Platinov's glowing face, shining brighter than the gold medal that hung around her neck, and the tears of helplessness filled his eyes once more.

Taking the photograph from the wall, he dropped it into the trash. He had had but two loves in his long, lonely life—Marynka Platinov and the Soviet Union. In the next seventy-two hours he would lose one of those loves.

He didn't intend to lose the other.

BOLAN ROSE from the floor and turned to Platinov. Behind the distant, deadpan expression on her face he saw the naked fear that radiated from her eyes.

"We've been exposed," she said blankly.

"Yes. We have seventy-two hours before we'll have to be quarantined."

The Russian woman nodded. "Then we must work quickly."

Through the window Bolan saw Grimaldi exit the chopper and walk toward the house. The Executioner knocked on the glass, shook his head vigorously and pointed back to the helicopter. A puzzled look covered the ace pilot's face as he turned back.

Bolan hurried into the kitchen. In a drawer by the sink he found a box of plastic freezer bags and several rolls of masking tape. Handing one of the rolls to Platinov, he said, "Seal the windows." The KGB agent followed him back to the living room.

The Executioner dropped the metal vial into a bag and zipped the lock. Careful not to spill the green, mossy substance within the cardboard box, he folded it in two and placed it in another of the bags. Under the kitchen sink he found a box of black plastic trash bags. Shoveling the smaller bags inside, he twisted the top, then taped it tightly.

From the living room came the sounds of more masking tape being torn from the roll as Platinov secured the openings to the outside. Bolan took a deep breath. He didn't know how fast the Viryphus strain would spread, but at least they were out of the wind, inside the house. He'd have to hope that their efforts to isolate the disease would be effective until experts arrived.

Bolan pushed the trash bag under the sink and closed the door. Stepping over a dead JRA gunner in the doorway, he walked down the hall to the living room.

Platinov stood next to the telephone.

The warrior frowned. Another of her mysterious reports? He could understand orders to advise her superiors as to their progress. What made the phone calls suspicious was her timing. He was always conveniently out of the room.

"Are you finished?" he asked.

Platinov nodded. "Almost. Two more windows and the door."

"We'll get the door after we're out." Bolan walked to the window.

The helicopter sat in a vacant lot next to the house, Grimaldi behind the controls. The chopper's landing hadn't impressed the jaded, wine-drinking revelers that still lined the streets. And the shots from inside the house had paled in comparison to the fireworks exploding from the streets and bullring.

Bolan walked back to the phone. The plastic covering had cracked down the middle, the victim of a stray round. The instrument still functioned, and he gave the overseas operator the President's emergency mission number. He waited, clicks sounding in his ear as the line was routed.

Briefly the Executioner ran down the situation and gave the President directions to the house. "So far I think we've gone unnoticed. But it's only a matter of time before someone gets nosy, and anyone searching the house not only risks contamination, but setting the Viryphus strain loose. Get some people who know what they're doing over here. And someone to stand guard."

"Immediately." The President cleared his throat. "Does this mean that you and Platinov have been exposed?"

"It does. I'll be in touch, sir." Bolan hung up.

He glanced toward the corner where the metal vial had lain. The same uneasy feeling he'd gotten in Sitges was back. He scanned the room. As at the cliff house, something was wrong—out of place—not as it should be...but what?

Slowly he crossed the room to the corner. Stooping, he lifted a piece of the shattered pottery. The Executioner frowned as he held it to the light streaming through the window. It was similar to the pieces he'd seen at the cliff house in Sitges. Clay. He was no archaeologist, but even to the untrained eye it was obviously American Indian.

That was it.

Everything else in both houses had been manufactured locally. The furniture, kitchen utensils, everything in the houses had been functional items. The Indian pottery was part of a collection.

The Executioner scanned the room once more. More of the pottery, some in pieces, some still intact, was scattered on the tables and floor. He filled the pockets of his jacket with the pieces before selecting two medium-size pots from an end table.

Bolan and Platinov stopped on the porch to tape the door. They heard the helicopter engine crank over as they walked across the yard.

"Where do we go now?" Platinov asked as they boarded the chopper.

"Barcelona," Bolan answered. "To the Museum of Archaeology."

PLATINOV REACHED into her purse and brought out a compact as the chopper descended to the Barcelona airport. Opening the cover, she stared into the mirror and adjusted her makeup. None of them had spoken since Bolan had informed the pilot of what had happened inside the house.

The Russian woman glanced up at the man called Grimaldi. His face had turned a pallid gray, then taken on a cold, stony stoicism when he'd learned of their exposure to the disease.

Platinov turned her attention to the man at his side. Belasko sat straight-backed in his seat, betraying a military past. His eyes were glued to the chopper's windshield, his brows knitted in concentration. Shifting slightly in his seat, he turned to Grimaldi.

His words sent goose bumps rolling over her skin as they broke the silence. "Get the plane ready as soon as we land, Jack. I don't know where we're heading next, but I've got a hunch it's back home."

The pilot nodded.

She closed the compact. It was obvious that the two men had been friends for years.

The chopper touched down. Platinov followed Bolan to the terminal as they made their way quickly to the car rental counter. They had radioed ahead to reserve a vehicle, and the keys to the SEAT, a Spanish version of the Fiat, were waiting.

Once inside the car Platinov turned to him. "He's taking it hard."

Bolan shrugged. "We've been through the wars together."

"I can tell." She settled back in her seat as they pulled out of the parking lot and onto the highway leading north to Barcelona. Such friendships were few and far between in life. They were more valuable than gold. They were one of the few things that made life...worth living.

They reached the edge of the city, and Bolan looked quickly at the map on the seat between them. Platinov stared at him. The friendship between the big man and Grimaldi made her think of Colonel Rostipovitch. A faint grin curled her lips. Her relationship with Rotislav had been different. Yet in some ways it had been the same. The colonel had also served as a father figure.

Platinov felt her emotions calming as she took a small degree of comfort from the memory. She recalled the first day she'd met Rotislav Rostipovitch. As she'd sat in the grass stretching her hamstrings before practice, the old man had come wobbling onto the field.

The smile widened as she recalled the ill-fitting red sweat suit that bulged in all the wrong places on his pudgy body. He had introduced himself as a new assistant coach who would accompany the team to the Olympics in America.

Platinov suppressed a chuckle as they entered the city. Only a fool wouldn't have spotted him as the KGB plant that he was. His knowledge of track and field—of *anything* athletic—had quickly proved to be nonexistent.

Bolan stopped at a stop light and turned to her. "How do you feel?" he asked.

"It's almost like a dream. It doesn't seem real, but I must accept it. We both must. We must continue with our work." She paused, feeling the terror return. "Have you accepted it yet?"

He nodded. "A long time ago."

Platinov looked down at the hands in her lap. They felt numb. Momentarily her depth perception wavered and her fingers appeared to be far away. She closed her eyes, forcing her thoughts back to Rostipovitch.

The colonel had been in love with her. Although he had never told her as much, she had sensed his feelings. The trained KGB field operative in her might have missed them, but the woman in Marynka Platinov easily detected Rotislav's true intentions when he innocently squeezed her knee or accidentally brushed an arm across her breasts.

But he had behaved himself, never trying to take advantage of his power as her superior or her admiration of his abilities. And the old man's physical infatuation hadn't altered her veneration for him. He had been her mentor.

It had been Rotislav Rostipovitch who had convinced her there was life after sports. While she still wallowed in dark, gloomy despair after knee injuries ended her track career, it had been Rostipovitch who convinced her she could still serve her country. Perhaps even more efficiently than she had as an athlete.

She owed the man, and she'd do anything that Rotislav Rostipovitch asked of her.

As the SEAT continued down the streets of Barcelona, Platinov turned toward Bolan. Suddenly a multitude of conflicting emotions tumbled haphazardly through her soul. Could she *still* do anything that Rostipovitch commanded?

The big American pulled the SEAT to a halt in front of the Barcelona Museum of Archaeology. She watched him reach into the back seat and withdraw the cardboard box that contained the bowls and broken pieces of pottery.

A warm rush of camaraderie flooded through her. Like Grimaldi, she, too, had fought next to this man. She'd seen his prowess with a gun, his coolness under fire, his aptitude for battle strategy. He was by far the most superior warrior she had ever met.

The friendly feeling suddenly changed to a far more primitive and intimate emotion as Platinov watched Bolan exit the vehicle. She felt the blood race to her face as she followed him up the steps.

Could she kill Mike Belasko when the time came? The disciplined KGB officer in Marynka Platinov answered, "Yes."

The woman in her said nothing.

Bolan opened the door and ushered her inside the building. Platinov surveyed the foyer, noting the several pieces of Carthaginian sculpture that stood on pedestals within the hall. A uniformed guard, armed with a holstered revolver, sat dozing against the wall.

A short, reedy man in a tight European suit walked toward them, his heels clicking across the tile. Smiling at Platinov, he extended his hand to Bolan. "I am Señor Fraili, the curator. You are American?" Without waiting for a reply he asked, "Do you care to examine the museum on your own, or would you prefer a guide?"

"Maybe another time," Bolan said. Fraili tilted his head slightly, his eyebrows lowering. Bolan held up the box. "We've come across some interesting pieces, and we'd like someone to identify them."

"Ah," the little man said, "you're a collector?"

"In a sense."

"Come with me."

The clicking heels led them down the hallway through a huge room lined wall-to-wall with artifacts from Spain's Roman period. Turning down a narrow corridor, Fraili opened a door and waved them through into an office.

Bolan set the box on the desk. The curator looked up into his eyes. "May I?" he asked, indicating the box.

"Of course."

The man's delicate hands reached inside, and he withdrew several pieces of the broken pottery and placed them on the desk. "These didn't come from Spain," he said finally.

"No," Bolan replied, "I don't think so."

"I'm simply the curator and not an expert in these matters," Fraili continued. "But these appear, if I'm not mistaken, to come from your homeland. Well," the little man went on, "we must get someone who knows more about this than myself. And I think you may be in luck. There's an American professor on sabbatical who's with us this year. He's studying a link between the Iberians and your American Indians.'' Fraili replaced the pieces and lifted the box. ''If you'll follow me, please.''

Platinov followed Bolan and Fraili back down the hall to another, smaller office near the rear of the building. The curator opened the door and they stepped inside.

A bald head wearing wire-rimmed glasses shot up from the book on the table. An enormous turquoise nugget cinched the string bolo tie at the neck. The man's eyes drilled through Platinov's as his tongue shifted a huge lump of something from one cheek to the other before he spoke. ''I'm busy. What in Sam Hill do *you* want?''

''Señor Garrett, allow me to introduce Señorita Platinov and Señor Belasko. They wish you to examine something.'' He set the box on the desk. ''This is Doctor Dub Garrett of New Mexico State University. Professor Garrett is America's foremost authority on Indian artifacts.''

''Yeah,'' Garrett said, irritated. ''Like a bullfrog has wings.'' He rose slowly and extended his hand to Bolan. ''The only reason I'm on top is 'cause nobody else knows shit from wild honey.'' He scowled as they shook hands. ''What do you want?''

Bolan leaned forward, lifted the two bowls from the cardboard box and placed them on the table. He had placed three of the broken pieces next to them when Garrett held up his hand.

"Enough," the old man said.

Platinov frowned. "What are they?"

"Puye," Garrett answered.

"Puye? What is Puye?" Fraili asked.

"Indians," Garrett said in exasperation. "South-west United States. Most folks have at least heard of their cliff dwellings south of Taos. The accomplishments of their civilization go far beyond that, however." He paused. "I'm sorry," he said sarcastically, "but I don't have time to give you a free lecture."

A slight smile lifted Bolan's lips. "Can you tell us where these came from?"

Garrett sighed and picked up one of the larger pieces. "This broken recently?"

"Early today, as a matter of fact."

"Yes. Obvious. Pity." He studied the piece closely. "The only intact pieces of Puye work to be found in years were right there in the vicinity of the cliff dwellings. Had a dig there twenty...no, thirty years ago. Money for the project ran out." Garrett paused, walked around the table and let a huge glob of brown spittle fall out of sight toward the floor.

Platinov heard a brassy ring as the tobacco juice hit metal. Out of the corner of her eye she saw Fraili wince.

"Rumor had it there was more to be found, though. If I was a bettin' man, that's where I'd say these come from." Garrett resumed his seat behind the table. "Now I don't mean to be rude, and I'm sure you think whatever you're up to is worth doin', but it don't affect me, and I got some damn important work to do myself.'' He waved his hand toward the door.

''It might affect you more than you think,'' Bolan said as they moved toward the door. ''And believe it or not, you've just done the most important bit of work you're ever likely to do.''

7

The Puye Cliff Dwellings were located just outside Espanola, New Mexico, twenty-five miles north of Santa Fe. Unlike similar pueblos such as Bandelier National Monument to the south, Puye hadn't been defiled with concrete ramps and railings to assist tourists in their exploration. With the exception of the log office building at the cliff's base, the three levels of dwellings remained almost entirely as they had centuries ago when they'd served to house the ancient tribe of North Americans.

Bolan turned off the highway and pulled the Suburban up the cracked concrete drive. The small parking lot was deserted except for a blue pickup bearing the New Mexico State seal, and a tar-stained Buick. A gravel path led the way to the office. A dusty dirt road disappeared around a curve to the east.

The Executioner reached into the back seat and grabbed his carryon. He removed two granola bars and handed one to Platinov. "Better eat while we can."

The Russian woman took the bar without speaking.

Glancing quickly over his shoulder, Bolan checked to make sure the blanket still hid the Uzis, M-16s and other equipment. The weapons pickup in Sitges had gone sour, and the Executioner had no intentions of losing this load of armament to thieves or the curious eyes of a park ranger.

The guns had been waiting for them when the B-1B touched down at Holloman Air Force Base near Alamogordo. Grimaldi had proven his indispensability once more with another short chopper jump north to Espanola. From there Bolan had taken the wheel of the rented four-wheel drive.

The Executioner pulled the keys from the ignition and stepped out into the early-morning humidity. Behind him he heard Platinov's door close, and a second later the Russian woman stood by his side.

Without speaking Bolan opened the door and ushered Platinov into the office building. A lone Indian male in his early twenties, his inky black hair dropping like a waterfall past his shoulders and down his back, stood impassively behind a glass counter. He shot an interested smile toward Platinov as she entered, the expression fading as Bolan followed her in.

As they neared the glass display counter, Bolan saw the mandatory T-shirts, baseball caps and bumper stickers advertising the dwellings.

The young man's grin returned. "Up early this morning." He took Bolan's twenty-dollar bill and opened the cash register. "Got the place all to yourselves—except for a father-and-son team who just went up."

Bolan nodded and slipped the change into a pocket of his jeans. He led Platinov out the door to the ancient brick steps that led to the first level of cave doors.

In the distance above them they could make out the movements of two figures, one larger than the other, as they made their way in and out of the openings.

"I suppose we must check every one," Platinov said, sighing as they made their way upward.

"I don't know any other way. You got anything better to do?"

Platinov chuckled. "With the last three days of my life? No. I suppose not." She paused, and Bolan could see the terror behind her smile. "What are we looking for?"

"Anything that might lead us to Musashi or another storage base."

"Should we split up?"

Bolan considered it. "No," he finally said. "We don't know what we're looking for. Two sets of eyes will mean we double-check everything."

A loud crack of thunder boomed over their heads as they neared the top of the primitive staircase. A few seconds later a light mist began to fall over the crude dwellings.

An unseen voice from the level above them echoed along the rocks. "Be careful, Jed! This rain'll make it slippery. You need to—"

"I know, I know," a younger voice answered impatiently.

Bolan stopped when he reached the top. The long row of entrances extended several hundred yards to the left, running what looked to be over a quarter mile in the opposite direction. The Executioner shook his head. "It'll take time."

The Russian woman faced away from the cliff, her eyes wide in astonishment at the endless miles of green-pined slopes below. "It is so beautiful," she said. "Someday when there's time I'd like to come back..." Her voice trailed off and the awe left her eyes. She turned to face him.

The Executioner didn't speak. He led the way to the end of the path, moving smoothly over the jagged rocks and dry soil. The sprinkle of rain halted as they made their way in and out of the small apertures.

Any artifacts that had once been inside the tiny rooms had long ago been removed to museums and the dens of collectors. With the exception of a small amount of graffiti defacing the walls, they found nothing to indicate that anyone had been inside for centuries.

As they neared the end of the first level, they saw the man and boy above them climbing a rough log ladder to the third tier. Closer now, Bolan could see that the father and son were dressed identically in white Puye T-shirts, cutoff jeans and gray hiking boots.

The father's voice came drifting down the side of the cliff. "Hold on, pal."

"Great idea, Dad." The boy laughed. "I hadn't thought of *that*."

As the morning drew on, the sun peeked through the clouds to heat the clammy air around them. By the time they'd finished searching the second level, Bolan's blue chambray work shirt clung to his skin.

He followed Platinov up the ladder to the last level of dwellings. The Russian woman had opened the last several buttons of her own work shirt, tying the ends in a knot beneath her breasts to expose rock-hard abdominal muscles below the skin.

As they continued in and out of the caves, the sun suddenly ducked back behind the clouds and more thunder roared over their heads. The drizzle returned, gradually escalating into a downpour to turn the dusty soil beneath their feet a deep brown.

Two steps ahead of him Platinov's foot slipped on a glistening rock, and the Executioner reached forward, grabbing her under the arms as she teetered dangerously close to the hundred-foot drop. Regaining her balance, she turned to face him, her eyes red and wet. Then, suddenly throwing her arms around his shoulders, she buried her face in his chest. "I don't want to die," she sobbed.

Gently Bolan slipped a finger under her chin and raised her eyes to meet his. He nodded. "None of us do."

Platinov stared up at him, tears streaking down her cheeks to mix with the rain. "Yes. And people like us must be prepared for death. I thought that I was, but I'm not. Not this kind of death."

Bolan wrapped her in his arms and hugged her closer. "We don't get to choose, do we?"

Thunder cracked like giant rifles in the skies, and they stood in the rain wrapped in each other's arms. Bolan pushed Marynka Platinov to arm's length as the water ran down his face, and nodded toward the nearest opening. "Let's wait it out."

Arm in arm they walked over the stones to the small door that had been carved in the rock centuries before their births. Once inside, Platinov untied the dripping shirt and stripped it over her head. She turned to Bolan, hands on her hips. Without speaking she unzipped her shorts and stepped out of them, standing nude in her hiking boots and socks.

Bolan looked her in the eye as she came to him. The musky dampness of wet skin mixed with perfume rose to his nostrils as she reached forward to unfasten his jeans. Leaning forward on her toes, she kissed him lightly, then her tongue shot from between her teeth, exploring his mouth as she hungrily pressed her lips harder against his.

Breaking the kiss, Platinov dropped to her knees in front of him and lowered his zipper. As her hand wrapped firmly around Bolan's rigid flesh, she said, "We can't continue our search until the rain stops, and our clothes have to dry." She looked up at him, her drenched hair clinging to her face, her eyes now intense with life. "And we may never have another chance."

TINY DROPLETS of water fell from the ladder as Bolan climbed past the last row of cliff dwellings. The sun had come out shortly after he and Platinov had finished their frenzied, impromptu lovemaking, and its furious rays now beat unmercifully against the back of his neck as he led the way to the top.

Stepping off the ladder to the rugged terrain of the flat plateau, Bolan turned to watch Platinov as she pulled herself up the rungs. The Russian woman had lain peacefully for a few minutes when they'd finished, then, as new rays of light drifted into the ancient dwelling, she'd risen quickly and dressed, becoming once again the serious professional with a mission to accomplish.

Bolan helped her to the top and turned to face the table of rock. Fifty yards away, in the center of the broad mesa, he saw the top rungs of a ladder peeking out from the Puye's ceremonial *kiva*.

On the other side of the opening, the father-and-son team stood, bare-chested, facing each other in martial arts stances. As Bolan and Platinov walked toward them, the boy, around twelve, skipped toward his father and launched a side kick. The father blocked and stepped to one side. "You're telegraphing," he said.

The boy stepped back and nodded.

They continued to spar as Bolan led the way down the ladder into the cool, damp room. The sun streamed down through the opening to form a round spot of light on the floor below. Bolan dropped to the dry, dusty stone and turned as Platinov descended.

Quietly they circled the empty room, scanning the walls and floor for any clue to the Japanese Red Army's presence.

"What was this place?" Platinov finally said, breaking the silence.

"A ceremonial chamber used for religious services. Sacrifices to the gods, things like that."

He saw Platinov frown in the shadows. "Human sacrifices?"

"Maybe. I don't know. I'm not a historian."

Climbing back to the top, they made their way across a dirt road that bisected the plateau. Water from the recent downpour had gathered in the tire-tracked path. Bolan turned back, gazing down the cliff. The road leading from the parking lot to the east evidently wound around the side of the cliff and up an unknown route to the top.

As they neared the man and boy, Bolan saw their wet T-shirts drying on a cluster of rocks. The father smiled at them as they approached, sweat dripping from under the bandanna he'd tied around his forehead. He continued to block his son's punches and kicks. "Kid's gettin' almost too good for me," he puffed.

"Almost, *nothing,*" the boy replied with a grin.

The shirtless man blocked a reverse punch from his son and tapped the boy lightly in the ribs with a roundhouse kick. "Gotcha."

"No, you didn't," the boy said quickly.

Bolan saw Platinov smile next to him. "They're friends, as well as family, yes?"

Bolan smiled back. "It looks that way."

The hot New Mexico sun crept once more behind the clouds. Bolan and Platinov arrived at the back edge of the cliff. Peering down, they saw the dense jungle of piñon pines, grassy undergrowth and plant vines that separated the cliff from another plateau across the valley. Bolan felt Platinov reach out and take his arm, then self-consciously drop it again.

He turned toward her, but she stared down to the valley below. "We've found nothing."

Bolan shook his head. "We've missed something. There's something here. I can feel it."

Platinov nodded somberly. "Yes. But will we have time to find it?"

The Executioner didn't answer. He looked at his watch. She was right. Each ticking second brought both of them—and the rest of the world—closer to death at the hands of this strange new disease.

The warrior had resigned himself to impending death long ago when he'd first launched his everlasting one-man war. He had known from the beginning that someday the odds wouldn't fall in his favor and he'd drop beneath a bullet or blade.

So now, as the end grew near, he hadn't experienced the shock that Platinov obviously felt.

His eyes moved across the valley to the cliff wall in the distance. In the large spectrum of things the manner in which a man died mattered little. How he lived, what difference he'd made during his allotted time was what was crucial.

"What do we do?" Platinov asked.

"Keep looking."

Bolan's eyes swept the valley below, dividing the mass of green into quadrants and systematically moving left to right through each sector. As the sun crept once more from behind the clouds, a quick flash of yellow winked back at him from between the tangled limbs. The Executioner's eyes returned to the spot, but the bright flicker had vanished. Fixing his gaze, he walked slowly to the side and the yellow color glimmered once more.

"What do you see?" Platinov asked.

"Metal." He turned back to where the man and his son were beginning to descend the ladder. "Stay here," he told Platinov, "and make sure no one comes down. If I saw what I think I saw, we're in business again.''

The Executioner began to descend the steep slope. Rain had muddied the dusty earth around the rock and gravel beneath his feet, and he held tightly to the tree limbs to keep from sliding. As he made his way through the branches and intermingled vines, the patch of bright yellow grew.

Using a large pine as cover, Bolan peered around the side. The front half of a yellow Ditch Witch trench digger sat half hidden under a pile of limbs. He crawled farther down the slope, stopping behind the Ditch Witch. A deep drainage channel had been cut into the valley floor. The recent water from the thundershower ran through the ditch, downhill toward the east.

Bolan heard a thud from somewhere in the opposite direction. He listened and detected soft footsteps on the pine needles. A moment later the same thud sounded again.

Dropping to his hands and knees, the Executioner catfooted forward, following the drainage ditch upstream toward the sounds. The periodic thuds and footsteps grew louder as he neared a small clearing.

Bolan stopped behind another thick pine and lifted his head to look through limbs and vines into the clearing. Facing the other way, a man wearing olive-green fatigue pants and a pale blue tank top walked slowly in the direction of a tiny opening in the rock wall. A white headband was knotted at the back of the man's neck; a Chinese Kalashnikov assault rifle hung from his shoulder.

The man turned suddenly and raised a long throwing knife over his head. Bolan saw the Oriental features of the sneering face, and the red Rising Sun on the headband, as the man sent the knife flipping through the air to sink into the tree.

The Executioner dropped back into the undergrowth as the JRA terrorist strode forward to retrieve the weapon. Burrowing down into the grass and vines, he watched as the terrorist jerked the blade from the tree trunk overhead.

An angry Japanese voice pierced the stillness. Bolan risked a quick glance from behind the tree.

Another Oriental, short and stocky, stood in the opening to the rocks. He shook his finger angrily at the knife thrower. The man in the headband resheathed his knife and hurried forward. Both men dropped to their knees and crawled into the cliff.

Bolan studied the tiny entrance. It had to have been a last-ditch hiding place for the ancient tribe who lived above, a place of refuge should their stronghold in the cliffs be overrun.

Centuries later the hideout at the bottom of the valley still offered seclusion and hiding. This time to the Japanese Red Army.

Bolan rose and turned from the tree. Quickly he made his way back up the slope.

THE SUBURBAN BUMPED up the rocky road to the top of the cliff dwellings. Bolan cut the engine and set the emergency brake. He turned to Platinov. "Saddle up."

The Russian woman's eyebrows lowered. "What?"

"Get ready."

Bolan stepped out of the vehicle and pulled the seat forward. Pulling the blanket off the equipment on the back seat, he slipped into the battle harness and fastened the tie-downs to his belt.

The suppressed Beretta 93-R already rode in shoulder leather under his light bush vest. The mighty Desert Eagle rode leather on the warrior's right thigh. Bolan slung an Uzi over his shoulder and filled the pockets of the vest with extra magazines. He watched silently as Platinov strapped a black nylon web belt around her hips, fastening it just below the buckle of the pack she already wore. She snapped the holster's safety strap over her H&K squeeze-cocker. The KGB agent grasped the slide of her Colt Woodsman between thumb and index finger and pulled gently rearward. A tiny, brass-encased .22 Hornet peeked out of the opening. She twisted lightly on the long suppressor screwed into the barrel. Satisfied that the weapon was ready, she slid it into her own shoulder rig, pulled an M-16 from the seat and checked the action.

Bolan attached the sheath of the Moran-Warner Bowie to his battle harness. The eight-and-a-half-inch blade was a good compromise between machete and knife. He might need the slashing capabilities of a longer blade once he encountered the dense foliage below. But a longer edged weapon would hamper the approach he'd planned.

"I still think we should cross the valley together," Platinov said as the Executioner pulled the rope and rappeling gear from the back of the 4x4. She reached in next to him, finding the Cold Steel All Terrain Chopper.

"No way," Bolan said. "We know nothing, absolutely nothing, about what we're up against. There could be a dozen guards posted in the valley down there. Just because I didn't see them on the way down doesn't mean they're not there. And we may find another hundred terrorists inside."

"That's unlikely."

"Unlikely, but possible. And I don't intend to get caught short if the long shot pays off. If one of us gets taken out before we reach the entrance, there's no point in the other one going down, too."

He watched Platinov strap the giant fourteen-inch chopper to her web belt. "Just follow the directions I gave you." He reached forward, raised her wrist to his eyes and looked at her watch. "Give me fifteen minutes lead time, then start down. You ought to get to the opposite wall about the same time I do. If you beat me, stay put and watch the rocks overhead." The Executioner slung the rope over his shoulder. "And remember. I want to take as many of them alive as we can. Time's getting short. We've got to find Musashi himself instead of chasing down these isolated storage bases."

He took off across the stony mesa, jogging carefully over the craggy rock. The valley to his side swept gradually upward, and when it finally rose to the plain, he climbed sideways down the gentle slope to the ground.

Reaching the back mesa, the Executioner found a trail leading upward. Ten minutes later he stood above the cliff wall that dropped down to the hidden entrance below. Anchoring his rope around a scrubby pine near the wall, he snapped the aluminum carabiners and figure eight in place, walked to the edge and leaned back, testing the friction. Then, taking a quick look at the heavy jungle of trees below, he shoved off.

Halfway down the rock wall, he encountered the first of the treetops crowding the face of the cliff. Maneuvering through the branches as best he could, he continued on toward the valley floor below.

The Executioner was thirty feet from the ground when he heard the voices. Twisting slightly on the end of the rope, he turned to face the dense forest. A faint patch of blue flashed through the trees. A woman with a heavy accent spoke rapidly and was answered by a short, terse spatter of Japanese.

The Executioner dropped lower and peered through the branches. Platinov, unarmed, stood facing the man in the light blue tank top. The JRA man held an AK-47 in his right hand and Platinov's M-16 in his left. Both the H&K squeeze-cocker and Colt had been shoved into the waistband of his fatigue pants.

Slowly Bolan reached for his Beretta and pulled it gingerly from the holster, the whisper of metal against leather seeming thunderous in the stillness. He watched as the JRA man thrust the AK-47 barrel into Platinov's back and prodded her ahead of him toward the opening. As they neared, the warrior unsheathed the Moran-Warner with his left hand. Hanging free at the end of the rope, he waited as his body spun slowly in the air. When the spinning stopped, he reached overhead, cutting halfway through the thick climbing rope.

The rope jerked, dropping him another two inches as the frayed ends began to snap and unwind. He saw Platinov glance quickly overhead, her eyes meeting his as she walked ahead of the terrorist. Slowly and carefully she gave an almost imperceptible nod.

Twisting and spinning on the end of the unraveling line, Bolan leveled the Beretta on a spot two feet from the opening. Platinov passed under the sights and dropped to her knees.

The JRA man barked in Japanese, and she leaned forward on all fours, preparing to crawl into the opening. Bolan braced a foot on the rock to his side. Still rotating slightly, he waited until the Beretta's sights fell on the blue tank top and squeezed the trigger.

The 93-R coughed softly and sent a 9 mm round streaking through the terrorist's shirt, just to the side of his heart. An instant later the Warner-Moran flashed over the Executioner's head, severing the remaining strands of rope. As he fell through the air, Platinov rolled to the side. The Japanese gave an astonished shriek and looked up. His last sight was the descending blade.

Bolan withdrew the thick Bowie from the man's chest, cut the climbing harness from his own body and silently dragged the man to the side of the entrance. Platinov replaced the H&K and Colt in her holsters. She glanced at the M-16, then reached down for the dead man's AK-47. She grinned at Bolan.

"Feel more at home now?" the Executioner whispered.

"It's Chinese rather than Russian," she answered softly, "but it'll do."

The Executioner dropped to his knees and crawled through the opening. A short hallway led inside the cliff to a sharp turn. They continued on and peered around the edge.

The crawl space opened into a large chamber. From somewhere within the cavern, out of sight to the side, the sound of voices echoed off the stone walls.

Bolan ducked back around the edge. The defense strategy behind the cave was obvious. One large, single room to temporarily house hundreds of Puye from their enemies. A few warriors, carefully placed here in the crawl space, could have systematically executed any unwanted heads that poked their noses inside.

The Executioner sat back against the wall, listening to the voices. That same strategy would have worked well for Musashi's terrorists. They could have put a bullet through both Bolan's and Platinov's heads the moment they showed their faces. Instead, the bored guard had opted to entertain himself with knife-throwing practice.

Bolan and Platinov crawled slowly down the hallway to the main entrance. Holding the Uzi at ready, the Executioner peered around the edge. The cavern was a hundred feet high and twice as deep and as wide. Large, naked spotlights hung from the ceiling on wires, and in the dim glow that covered the rear wall Bolan could see the outlines of another small hole. Scattered across the floor to the right were a dozen striped mattresses, where two men lay snoring. Remnants of fast-food take-outs, beer and soda cans littered the floor between the makeshift beds.

To the side of the mattresses four more JRA men sat at a folding card table, cursing in Japanese as they played mah-jongg. None of the terrorists appeared armed, but weapons—assault rifles, submachine guns and pistols—lay haphazardly around the room within reach.

Bolan turned back to Platinov. "We can take them alive," he whispered. "Follow me in."

The Executioner stepped through the door, bringing the Uzi up to bear at the end of the sling. "Freeze!" he shouted, the word echoing throughout the cave. He saw Platinov dart through the opening to take her position ten feet to his right.

The four men at the table looked up in shock, their hands frozen around the mah-jongg pieces. The man with his back to the door started to turn, and Bolan fired a shot burst over his head. "Stand up," he ordered.

No one moved.

"Someone here speaks English. And he'd better translate—fast. Stand up and keep your hands in plain sight."

The men remained motionless.

Bolan fired a burst between the mah-jongg players, cutting through the thin pasteboard table and sending the remaining tiles dancing through the air. He turned the Uzi toward the mattresses and squeezed again, shattering a wine bottle and scattering cans and papers across the floor.

All six men shot to their feet, hands in the air.

The warrior lined them up in the middle of the room. The stocky man he'd seen earlier, outside the cave with the knife thrower, said something to Platinov in Russian. Bolan heard the words but couldn't make them out. A second later the stock of Platinov's assault rifle cracked against the man's temple, dropping him to the floor.

"Not a bad idea," the Executioner said. "Lie down, hands spread to your sides."

The remaining five men joined their friend on the rocky floor. Bolan turned to Platinov. "You know him?"

The KGB major nodded. "From before."

Bolan nodded. Turning back to the reclining men, he said, "We're going to have a little talk."

The words had barely left his mouth when he saw the glitter of chrome steel at the end of the line. A man with a long black ponytail jerked to his knees, a nickel-plated .38 appearing in his hand. The hidden weapon jumped as he fired off balance, sending a wild round past Bolan that ricocheted around the cavern.

Bolan pivoted on the balls of his feet, squeezed the Uzi's trigger and drilled a 3-round burst into the terrorist's chest. The rest of the men rolled to their hands and knees, scampering for the weapons strewn around the room.

From the corner of his eye he saw Platinov drop to one knee. A tall, lanky JRA gunner fell under a long stream from her Kalashnikov.

"I not fight! I not fight!" a shrill voice screamed around the sounds of ricochets and gunfire. Bolan glanced to his side, seeing one of the men still prostrate on the floor, his hands clasped behind his neck covering his head.

A barrage of automatic fire sang past the Executioner's ear, and he dived to the ground, skidding along the gritty stone floor. He looked up to see a scowling face under another of the Rising Sun headbands. The man struggled to correct the aim of the Steyr AUG in his hands. Behind the man a terrorist wearing a black fatigue shirt turned and broke toward the opening at the rear of the cavern.

Bolan rolled onto his side as new rounds chipped the rock next to him. Squeezing the trigger of the small subgun, he fired a quick volley into the neck and face of the man in the headband.

Platinov's empty Kalashnikov locked open, and the KGB agent dropped it and drew the squeeze-cocker from her hip. She sent a double-tap of 9 mm autos drilling through the terrorist with the black fatigue shirt. The man spun full circle as he reached the small hole at the rear of the cavern, then dropped to the ground, half in, half out, of the opening.

As the dust settled and the roaring echoes quieted within the cave, the frightened voice on the floor screamed again, "I not fight! I not fight!"

Bolan jumped to his feet. "Check the others," he called to Platinov over his shoulder as he walked quickly to the man on the floor.

Holding the Uzi at arm's length, he pressed the barrel against the back of the terrorist's head and patted him down. Finding no weapons, he reached down and grabbed an arm. "On your feet and start talking."

"My English not so—"

"We'll make do. Where's Musashi?"

There was a long pause. "I do not know."

Bolan stepped forward and drew the mammoth Desert Eagle from his side. Popping the magazine from the .44, he held it to the JRA man's face.

The terrorist's eyes widened, his lower lip dropping as he saw the size of the Magnum rounds.

Slamming the mag back into the gun, Bolan said, "You've got three seconds. One."

"I . . . do not . . ."

"Two," Bolan growled.

The JRA man shook his head violently.

"Three."

The terrorist closed his eyes tightly and fell to the ground, unconscious.

Platinov joined Bolan. "They're all dead. This one?"

"He doesn't know anything. If he did, he'd have talked."

Platinov nodded. "It's just possible..." She turned to Bolan. "He appears willing to talk?"

Bolan nodded. "He appears to be aware of what will happen if he doesn't. Why?"

"Because..." Platinov's voice trailed off as she slid her pack around to the front and unzipped the zipper. "He may know more than even he believes." Reaching inside, the KGB agent produced a small vial of yellowish fluid and a syringe. She turned back to Bolan. The smile widened and her voice took on a mock dramatic air. "Comrade Belasko, in the Soviet Union *ve have vays to make zem talk.*"

8

Bolan pulled the terrorist to his feet and shoved him into a chair while Platinov uprighted the card table. Taking a plastic flex-cuff from his vest, the Executioner looped the strip around the man's wrists and secured his hands behind him. "Don't move," he ordered.

The frightened man nodded.

Platinov slid out of her shoulder rig and web belt and dropped them onto the table next to her pack. She pulled the Chopper from its sheath.

The terrorist's eyes stretched the sockets as Platinov walked toward his chair. He relaxed again as she replaced the long knife after cutting the sleeve from his shirt.

Platinov jammed the syringe into the vial and withdrew the liquid. "What . . . what are you doing?" the man asked, horror returning to his face.

"Don't worry," Platinov said. "It's only a mixture of sodium pentothal and a few other drugs."

"What other drugs?"

"It isn't important. There are no side effects to concern you. A slight headache perhaps—later— nothing more. The solution works somewhat like hypnosis. It will enable you to recall things you've forgotten.'' The terrorist winced slightly as she inserted the needle into his arm.

"I'll need quiet," Platinov said, turning to Bolan. "Isolation, if the drug is to be effective.''

Bolan walked to the cavity at the rear of the cave. Stepping over the corpse in the opening, he looked in to see a small five-by-five room.

A private area for the Puye chief perhaps. Whatever the room's original purpose, it would serve well for the interrogation Platinov was about to conduct.

A threadbare sofa and two folding chairs had been squeezed into the opening. More scattered food wrappings littered the floor.

Bolan dragged the man in the fatigue jacket to the side and retraced his steps to the card table. The terrorist's eyelids had fallen to half-mast as he took the man's arm and led him to the smaller room.

Platinov followed them in, positioning the groggy man on the sofa. She dropped into one of the chairs.

Bolan returned to the main cavern and scanned the vast room. The Japanese Red Army guards had led a Spartan existence inside the cliff. Besides the mattresses and card table, the cave held little to add to human comfort. Three large OD green footlockers sat against a side wall, and the Executioner walked toward them, passing a bundle of pornographic magazines strewn about the floor.

Platinov's voice drifted into the cavern as he opened the lid of the first locker. "What is your name?" the Russian woman asked.

"Egawa," came the sluggish reply. "Akira Egawa.''

The footlocker contained more weapons—rifles and shotguns. Bolan closed the lid and moved to the next trunk as Platinov methodically asked insignificant, preliminary questions. He found extra magazines for the rifles and boxes of ammunition in various calibers stacked in the second locker.

"Where were you born?" he heard Platinov ask as he opened the lid of the final trunk.

"Osaka."

The third trunk contained a pile of oily rags and a gun-cleaning kit. Bolan lifted them to reveal a thick steel fire box, the key still in the lock. Setting it on the floor, he dropped one knee to the cool stone.

The Executioner twisted the key, and the lid sprang partially open on its hinges. He lifted a long metal cylinder, identical to the one they'd found in Sitges, from the box.

Bolan closed the lid and relocked the box. Taking it and the gun-cleaning kit with him, he returned to the card table and took a seat.

"What was your mother's name, Akira?" Platinov asked.

"Sachiko."

"Where are you now?"

"America."

"Where in America?"

"New Mexico."

"And where in New Mexico?"

"I do not know."

From behind the rock Bolan heard Platinov sigh quietly. "Yes, Akira," she said. "You do know. You must think."

"I do not know. We were driven here at night. I slept."

Bolan opened the gun-cleaning kit and slid the Beretta from under his vest. He unscrewed the suppressor as Platinov continued, her voice calm and soothing.

"Think, Akira. Somewhere along the way you awakened."

"Yes."

"And while you were awake you saw something. Or you heard something. Something that will enable you to further pinpoint your location. What was that something?"

Silence came from the smaller room as Bolan broke down the Beretta and began rubbing a solvent-soaked rag over the pieces. He had begun applying a thin coat of oil to the weapon when Egawa finally answered.

"A sign...I saw a road sign," the man's sleepy voice said. "Espanola."

"And what else?" Platinov asked.

"The elevation. But I do not remember it."

"Yes, you do remember, Akira. You must remember. Picture the sign in your mind. What did it say?"

"It said 5,585 feet."

Bolan reassembled the Beretta. He reached for Platinov's Heckler & Koch, pressed the slide retainer at the rear of the frame and dismantled the weapon. He glanced momentarily at the H&K's innards. The squeeze-cocking device was a radical new innovation, replacing the need for a safety. Unless the cocking panel at the front of the grips was pressed firmly inward, the weapon wouldn't fire.

The Executioner began wiping down the squeeze-cocker as Platinov's questions became more pertinent.

"Do you know where Musashi's base camp is located?"

"No."

"Think, Akira. Somewhere you have heard things . . . seen things. . . ."

Silence filled the cavern as Bolan finished cleaning the squeeze-cocker. He'd begun stripping the Uzi when Egawa finally answered.

"Hokkaido. Junko said Hokkaido."

"Where on Hokkaido?"

"I do not know."

"Think."

Bolan cleaned and reassembled the Uzi and placed it on the table next to Platinov's pack. He reached for the Colt Woodsman in the KGB agent's shoulder holster, then looked back at the pack.

"Barracks," Egawa said. "Underground barracks."

"How do you know this?"

"A telephone conversation. Musashi was talking to someone—I do not know who. They were preparing the base. Readying it for occupation." The terrorist paused, then continued, his voice slow and sluggish. "Musashi laughed as he spoke, saying that the new base was invisible. Even from the air."

"What did that mean?"

"I do not know. But it was once a Japanese air base. I recall him saying that."

Bolan reached out, unzipped the pack and opened the flap. Digging through the contents, he found two extra H&K magazines and a box of 9 mm ammunition. He put them on the table.

At the bottom of the pack was a hard rubber case. Through the clear plastic of the cover another syringe was visible. Next to it rested a vial, identical to the one from which Platinov had drawn the interrogation drug.

"Where on Hokkaido is the base? Think, Akira."

"I will think."

The smaller room fell silent again as Bolan lifted the rubber case and eyed the vial. The liquid in it was slightly darker than the fluid the KGB agent had inserted into the JRA man's arm.

The terrorist spoke again, slowly, his voice trailing from the smaller room into the open cavern. "Musashi said Sapporo many times during the conversation. Supplies would be purchased at Sapporo." Egawa paused again. "Junko said they would be isolated—except for the mongrels."

"Who are the mongrels, Akira?"

"The Ainu."

Bolan thought briefly of the still half-wild race that occupied the northern island in Japan. Caucasian in origin, they were held on reservations by the Japanese, much like the American Indians in the United States.

"Where on Hokkaido is the camp?" Platinov repeated. "Think, Akira."

The Executioner turned his attention back to the empty pack. He lifted it by the flap and the bottom sagged, bunching in the middle. Bolan frowned, set-

ting it back on the table and running his hand inside.
His fingers stopped as they encountered a long, narrow lump at the bottom of the pack. Holding the
black nylon up to the light, he saw the faint outline of
a zipper hidden beneath the seam.

In the smaller room Bolan heard Platinov change
tracks. "Tell me about the air base," she said. "How
is it entered?"

"Through the third hangar. The rest of the entrances have been sealed."

Bolan unzipped the zipper and reached inside. A
sick feeling swept through him as his fingers told his
brain what they'd found. The Executioner pulled one
of his own granola bars from the hidden compartment. The paper had been carefully unwrapped at
both ends.

"Where does the entrance lead?"

"To the Doomsday room. Musashi calls it the
Doomsday device."

"What does Doomsday mean, Akira?"

"Hokkaido. Junko said Hokkaido."

"We have covered that, Akira. What does Doomsday mean?"

"I will think."

Bolan lifted the plastic cover from the rubber case
and unscrewed the vial. The odor of bitter almonds
assaulted his nostrils as he held the vial to his nose.

Arsenic.

The Executioner turned toward the opening at the
rear of the cavern. Arsenic. It was the perfect choice
under the circumstances. The nuts in his granola bar
would camouflage the taste of the almonds. At worst

he might think he'd bitten into a stale bar. And by injecting both ends with the poison, Platinov could ensure that even if he discarded the bar after the first bite, enough of the toxin would have entered his system to accomplish her objective.

Bolan reached into his vest, producing a felt-tipped pen. Carefully he placed a small black dot in the center of the *O* in the word *Granola* on the wrapper, then replaced the bar in the false bottom. Cautiously returning the contents as he'd found them, he stacked the magazines and ammunition over the rubber case and rezipped the pack.

"I do not understand how it works," Egawa said. "But if the base camp is attacked, Viryphus will be automatically dumped into the water system... somewhere."

Platinov's voice rose a note. "Where?"

"I do not know."

Bolan waited quietly, listening. Finally Egawa spoke again. "It is all I know. I am certain."

The Executioner returned the pack to the spot where Platinov had placed it. He stood and walked to the opening.

Egawa lay on his back on the sofa, his forearm resting over his eyes. He'd begun to snore lightly.

Platinov looked up, smiling, as the Executioner stepped into the room. "He's asleep," she whispered. "But I believe he's told us everything."

Bolan looked her squarely in the eye. "I know all *I* need to know."

THE EXECUTIONER hit the ground, rolled and sprang back to his feet, drawing hard on the lines to gather the chute in the strong Hokkaido wind. A quarter mile to the east he saw Platinov touch down and do the same.

Bolan folded the parachute and shoved it under a large rock, then turned toward the Russian woman, who was fighting to gain control of her own lines. He hadn't mentioned finding the granola bar in her pack. At this point *he* had the advantage. He knew what she intended to do and how she planned to do it. If he alerted the KGB agent that he was onto her alternate mission, she'd simply change tactics.

The Executioner patted the side pocket of his backpack, feeling the remaining granola bars through the thin nylon. There had been five bars remaining when he'd discovered the Russian woman's plan.

Somewhere, during the flight to Hokkaido, that number had grown to six. And one sported a black dot in the middle of the *O* on the wrapper.

Bolan walked toward Platinov as she folded her chute. He felt a twinge of remorse as he realized he might have to kill her in self-defense.

The Russian woman looked up as he neared. "The wind is strong."

He nodded and helped her anchor the parachute under a stack of small stones. That accomplished, they broke into double time as they crossed the plains of Japan's northernmost island. They'd planned to land less than a mile from the Ainu reservation, but the strong winds had diverted them. If his calculations were correct, they had almost three miles to cover before they reached their destination.

As they jogged past a dairy farm in the distance, Platinov broke the silence. "It looks like pictures I've seen of America," she said, timing the words with her breathing. "The plains states." She pointed toward the red gambrel-roofed barn. The round metal edge of a silo peeked from behind the western-looking building, and several Holstein cattle grazed contentedly in a nearby corral.

Bolan shifted the Uzi sling to his other shoulder as they ran. "At the turn of the century, shortly after they'd conquered the Ainu, the Japanese brought farm and dairy experts in from America to teach them the trade. They still send people to some of the U.S. agriculture schools." They slowed to a walk as they neared a wooded area. "The reservation should be just the other side of these trees," Bolan added.

Platinov shook her head as they made their way through the trees. "How do you know the Ainu will help us?"

"I don't," Bolan answered. "But they're our best bet. They're hunters—fishermen. They'll know the area better than anyone."

Coming to a small stream, they saw two modern steel traps surrounded by several older contraptions made of wood and twine. Stepping carefully over the devices, they moved on to the end of the woods.

Fifty feet from the edge of the trees was a short bamboo fence. A tall sign, painted in red *kanji* figures, towered over the poles. A hundred yards across the fence stood two dozen reed-thatched huts. A number of separate buildings, rising into the air on stilts, were off to the side. Ten-foot poles had been driven into the ground around the huts. At the top of the poles the bleached white skulls of animals shone brightly in the sunlight.

Bolan and Platinov crossed the fence. In the distance tiny figures moved in and out of the huts. As they neared, they saw a group of children running and playing with a black bear cub.

Two heads turned toward them as they crossed the flat land. Then the figures broke away from the village and walked to meet them.

"Are the Ainu friendly?" Platinov asked.

"We'll find out."

As the tiny figures grew larger, Bolan saw that both men had long, wavy black hair and beards. One man wore a woven bark-cloth kimono, the other a long furry skin-drape decorated with geometric designs. As the men drew nearer, the gray hair and wrinkled face under the Russian rabbit hat of the man dressed in skins became clear.

The two men stopped before them, eyeing their weapons. At close range Bolan could see that a thick mat of hair covered the arms and necks of both men. The older man spoke in a strange, agglutinative tongue, a few words of contemporary Japanese seeming out of place among the ancient utterances.

When neither Bolan nor Platinov responded, the younger man stepped forward, speaking Japanese.

Bolan shook his head.

"Perhaps they speak Russian," Platinov suggested. She tried.

They didn't.

The old man in the skins motioned for them to follow and turned on his heel, leading Bolan and Platinov to the village. Heads turned in amazement as they walked through the huts.

They stopped in front of a large dwelling near the center of the settlement. The old man waved the younger one away, speaking once more in the antiquated language. The younger man hurried off.

Bolan and Platinov followed the gray-haired man into a large living area within the hut. Wood carvings in the shapes of the sun, fire and lightning covered the walls. Hanging from the ceiling at the far end of the room were several rows of wooden sticks, their bark partially shaved and drooping in the air.

The old man yelled loudly. A moment later a younger man wearing blue jeans and a white cotton T-shirt appeared from a back room. The T-shirt bulged in clumps on the man's torso, and the same thick black body hair extended over the neck of the shirt and down his arms beneath the sleeves. He stared wide-eyed at Bolan and Platinov, then the stare broadened into a smile. Turning back to the doorway, he shouted excitedly in the strange language.

A moment later a woman carrying a baby crept uncertainly into the room. A dark tattoo simulating a mustache covered her upper lip.

"These people must like hair," Platinov whispered.

The smile on the young man's face widened further. "Yeah," he said, his voice a strange mixture of Texas drawl and the accent they'd heard when the other two Ainu spoke. "We're the hairiest folks on the face of the earth. Grab a seat.'' He motioned toward the mats on the floor.

Bolan and Platinov looked briefly at each other and sat down. Across from them the young man and his wife did the same. Opening her kimono, the tattooed woman began nursing the child. The gray-haired man's eyes were glued to Bolan and Platinov.

''My daddy,'' the younger man said, indicating the man in the rabbit hat. ''He ain't never seen a white man wasn't Ainu before.''

Bolan smiled. ''I can't help but wondering—''

''Where I learned English?'' the young man said. ''Spent four years at Texas A&M. Ag student.'' He leaned forward, extending his hand. ''Nobody there could pronounce my real name. Doubt if you can, either. So the Texans just changed it for me.''

''What do we call you?'' Platinov asked.

''Harry.''

Bolan shook his hand, suppressing a smile. Harry turned to Platinov. ''This the little woman?''

''No.'' Bolan went on before Harry could respond. ''Harry, I can't tell you who we are. Only that we're vitally interested in helping your people. Actually we're interested in helping all people against a threat that's even more serious to you than the Japanese. It's more serious than anything you've ever heard of— probably ever dreamed of. We don't have much time, and we need your help.''

Harry leaned forward, his brows lowering and the wrinkles across his forehead making him look more like his father.

"We're looking for a deserted Japanese fighter pilot base," Bolan said. "It's being occupied by members of a terrorist group known as the Japanese Red Army."

"So that's who those assholes are."

"You know where the base is?"

Harry rose from his seat. "Hell, yes. Everyone on the reservation does—the dumbshits in the hole just don't know we do. Hell, we hunt and fish all over that spread. It's just down the road a piece. Want me to take you there?"

"Please," Platinov said.

Harry disappeared into the back room and returned a moment later, wearing a maroon-and-white Texas A&M sweatshirt. He knelt on the mat, jammed his feet into a pair of round-toed cowboy boots and placed a ragged straw hat on top of his head. "How do I look?" He grinned at Bolan.

"Harry," he said, "just like a good ol' boy."

The Ainu beamed back in delight.

9

Bolan pressed the binoculars against his forehead and stared through the grove of trees across the plain. Musashi had been right, he thought. The former Japanese air base *was* invisible. At least from a distance.

Five concrete reinforced hangars rose from the ground, each surrounded and covered with grass and brush. Peeking through the camouflage around the hangar second from his right, the Executioner could see the corners of a side door. Just below the dusty glass window he saw faded paint in the shape of the number 4.

He turned the binoculars to the middle hangar. The brush had been cut into a narrow path leading to the door. He focused on the number beneath the window.

Hangar number three.

Besides the small side entrances, each hangar had a large sliding door that opened onto the cracked concrete runway. It was from these doors that the Japanese fighter planes had emerged for takeoff almost half a century ago. Of no apparent use to the base's new occupants, they'd been blocked and hidden with grass and dirt, as well.

Thick wooden poles surrounded the entire base, rising into the air to hold camouflage netting that concealed the runways from the air. Thirty feet aboveground the canopies stood amply high to allow planes to take off from beneath.

A quarter mile away Bolan watched through his field glasses, counting four camouflaged men patrolling the base perimeter. Each wore the distinctive Rising Sun headband.

The Executioner dropped the binoculars and turned toward the cowboy Ainu. He'd decided to trust Harry, explaining the situation fully as they'd made their way to the compound. The strange hybrid of ancient Oriental warrior and Texas cowboy had the benefits of both East and West. His insight might prove invaluable in the hours to come.

"They think we don't know about them," Harry drawled. "Not that it made a rat's ass bit a difference. Until now we just didn't care."

Bolan nodded. They faced a quarter mile of open terrain between them and the compound. He turned to Platinov.

The Russian agent read his mind. "It'll have to be tonight," she whispered.

Turning away from the base, they made their way back to the Ainu reservation.

"Have you got a telephone?" Bolan asked as they entered the village.

Harry nodded. "Take you to it."

Bolan and Platinov followed the Ainu up the dusty road separating the huts to a modern concrete building. They entered the door to find a row of ancient coin-operated washing machines and dryers.

One old woman, her lip tattooed like Harry's wife, was fumbling with a dryer. Harry said something in the ancient tongue, and the woman nodded, dropped her clothes and left the building.

Bolan walked to the pay phone in the corner. Harry handed him a coin, and he dropped it in the slot and dialed the mission hot line.

A minute later the President answered on the first ring. "Mack?"

Bolan wasted no time. "We've located Musashi's base."

"Yes?"

"We'll strike tonight. But we've learned of several complications. First, there's what Musashi calls a Doomsday feature. I don't know the details, but it's some type of device that will automatically release the Viryphus disease at an undisclosed location."

There was a long pause. "How do you plan to handle it?"

"We'll penetrate the base and disable the device."

The President cleared his throat. "Isn't that risky?"

"Sure it is," Bolan answered. "But considering the time element, we don't have another choice."

"What about the B-1B?" the President asked. "Couldn't Grimaldi strafe—"

Bolan interrupted. "The Doomsday device would more than likely be set off. Plus, we'd risk the chance of freeing the supply of the disease that's here. No, the device has got to be disabled before we're discovered.

But there's another problem of equal concern, and we'll need your help."

"Anything you say. Name it."

"So far communication between storage bases hasn't appeared to be strong," Bolan continued. "They've relied more on the remoteness and diversity of their locations for security. But there can always be an exception to the rule. If any, *any* of the other storage bases are alerted during our attack, they'll release the viral-bacteria. What I need you to do is contact the leaders of all the nations. Tell them to put their special units—GSG-9, Spetznaz, SAS—on alert. You do the same with Delta. There's got to be a list of the storage compounds somewhere inside. As soon as I locate it, I'll call you. Have some kind of central command where you can get them into action immediately." The Executioner drew a deep breath. "The guards we've encountered at the bases won't be any match for these units, but it's the clock we're fighting. Word of our attack will leak out, and I don't know how much time they'll have to neutralize the threat."

Bolan heard the President blow air from his lips into the mouthpiece. "That's cutting it close. It's a hell of a long shot, Mack."

"It's our only shot, Mr. President," Bolan said, and hung up.

Harry led them from the laundry building to a small, deserted hut. The Executioner dropped his weapons and pack onto the mat and sat down. He turned to Platinov as Harry left, promising to return a half hour before dusk.

Platinov took a seat and busied herself stripping and checking her weapons. She glanced up self-consciously now and then as Bolan studied her. Finally she laughed nervously. "Why do you watch me? Am I that beautiful?"

Bolan didn't answer. Unless he missed his guess, her orders had been to use him until the base was located, then kill him and take the Viryphus supply. Well, they knew where Musashi was now. If that was the case, she didn't need him anymore.

And in the battle that was about to take place, the KGB agent would have plenty of opportunities to turn her squeeze-cocker on him.

It was time to find out.

"Yeah," he said. "You *are* beautiful." He unzipped his backpack and pulled out the six granola bars. "Dinnertime. He divided the bars equally, handing her three and making sure she got the one with the dot.

Platinov reached out to take the bars. She smiled pleasantly and set them on the mat beside her. "I'm afraid I'm too nervous to eat."

Bolan unwrapped one of his bars. Holding it in his left hand, he kept his right close to the Desert Eagle as he took a bite.

Platinov returned her eyes to her weapons.

"Better eat," Bolan said. "We'll both need our strength."

The Russian woman laughed self-consciously. "I'll run on nervous energy. Besides—" her voice became sad "—in a few more hours it'll make no difference. To either of us."

Bolan finished his first granola bar and unwrapped the second. "That's not the point. The people of the world are counting on you. *I'll* be counting on you. It won't do to have you in a weakened condition."

Platinov didn't answer. She opened the slide of the Colt Woodsman, checked the round in the chamber and returned it to her shoulder holster.

Bolan finished the second bar and started on the third. "That one seemed a little stale. Probably the dry climate in New Mexico."

Platinov reached into her pack and removed the H&K magazines, checking to make sure the rounds were firmly seated against the spine.

"I hate to give you orders, Major. But I'm going to have to insist that you eat something."

Platinov slammed one of the magazines onto the mat, the lead round snapping from its place and rolling across the floor. "Damn you, Belasko," she said, tears rolling down her cheeks. "We're not all like you. I'm nervous. I'm upset. For God's sake, in a few hours I'll be dead!"

Bolan shrugged and finished his last granola bar. "Is that what's bothering you? Or is it the fact that I've finished eating. And I'm still alive?"

The color drained from the Russian woman's face. "What . . . what do you mean?"

Bolan slid the Desert Eagle out of its holster. "You know what I mean. One of these six granola bars has arsenic in it. And since I've finished mine, we know who has the lucky one."

Platinov slouched back on the mat, her shoulders dropping forward in exhaustion. "I . . . I couldn't do it,'' she whispered. She looked up, staring into his eyes. "Yes, I had my orders. But you must believe me. I violated those orders. I didn't do it." She paused and a lone tear dribbled from her eye to her chin. "And I won't do it," she added softly.

Bolan watched her. She was either telling the truth or was one hell of an actress. "Really? Great. Show me the vial."

Platinov stared back at him. "I threw it away. I didn't want to take the chance of changing my mind."

Bolan nodded. "How convenient. And I'm supposed to buy that?"

Platinov wiped the tear from her face. She looked down at the granola bars on the mat in front of her. Then, reaching forward, she tore the wrappers from all three bars and set them on the mat.

"Don't bother," Bolan said. "Just the one with the dot in the *O*."

The Russian woman lifted the first bar, inspected the wrapper beneath it, then set it back down. She checked the paper under the second bar, then held it up to show Bolan the tiny felt-tipped ink mark he had made in the cave in New Mexico. Slowly she bit off the end and began to chew.

Bolan waited.

When she finished, she looked up once more, the tears returning to her eyes. "Now do you believe me?"

The Executioner didn't answer. He shoved the Desert Eagle back into his holster and opened his arms to the weeping Russian woman.

MUSASHI MADE HIS WAY quietly through the underground corridors, his thoughts returning to his American contact as he neared the Doomsday room. The man hadn't called again. The JRA leader hadn't heard from him since the fiasco in Pamplona.

The American would pay dearly for his negligence.

Musashi grinned. Perhaps he'd pull the man's mustache from his lip, hair by hair, before he killed him. He'd never done that to a man before.

Musashi thought of Marynka Platinov. She was the only KGB official he had ever met face-to-face, during the days when the Soviets had provided funding and weapons to the JRA. Then the Soviet policy had changed. They no longer wanted the help of their terrorist friends around the world.

Good, Musashi thought. He no longer wanted *them*.

Musashi opened the door and peered into the Doomsday room. At the desk behind the screen Yuji's bald head jerked, then the chubby man relaxed as he saw the JRA leader in the doorway.

Musashi stood in the hall, holding the door as he spoke. "All goes well?"

"It's well," Yuji replied.

Musashi had started to close the door when he heard the doorway open in the hangar above them. A moment later Hiroshi and Kenji, both dressed in green-and-brown camouflage fatigues, walked wearily down the stairs. Seeing Musashi, the two men slung their Kalashnikovs over their shoulders and saluted.

Musashi nodded. "Have you anything to report?"

Kenji shook his head. "Nothing of importance. Three of the Ainu were spotted in the distance. They appeared to be watching the base."

Musashi snorted. "The mongrels are too stupid to understand what they've seen. They'll believe we're with the government. Even if they suspected something, who would believe the fleece-covered beasts?"

The two guards laughed and crossed the room, disappearing down the corridor.

"Alert me immediately if the call comes from America," Musashi told Yuji. "The time draws near. I don't wish to take chances. You can reach me on the intercom."

The bald man nodded, then turned back to the screen as Musashi closed the door.

The JRA man walked quietly down the hall, his straw *zoris* making soft, slapping noises as they flapped against his heels. Stopping at the laboratory, he stuck his head inside. Dr. Takahata stood at the counter, pouring another of his vile concoctions from a test tube into a dish. Musashi grinned to himself. Since losing the tip of his finger, the old man had worked like a dog. He hadn't yet perfected the cure for Viryphus, but with this pain-induced renewal of interest it was only a matter of time.

Musashi made a full tour of the underground complex, finishing at the exit to hangar number five. He turned back down the hall, assuring himself there were no curious eyes, then opened the fuse box in the wall and flipped switches four and six simultaneously.

The huge, round portal leading to the stairs swung open. Musashi flipped the switches back and the door swung closed once more. He gazed momentarily at the switches numbered five and seven. A similar act with these two would automatically sweep the brush and rubble from the front of the runway door above. The JRA leader smiled.

Every good strategist had a backup plan, and this secret escape exit was his. The rest of the JRA believed that all but hangar number three had been sealed off.

And the JRA man who had rigged the door, the same man who had set up the Doomsday device itself, had mysteriously disappeared.

Musashi shook his head. It had been a shame to have to kill him. The man had been a technological genius.

The JRA leader reached his room and unlocked the door. He replaced his swords in the rack and lay down on his mat, closing his eyes. A peaceful serenity replaced his melancholy as he thought of the days of glory to come. He'd decided to ask for more. The release of a few JRA soldiers was nothing. He craved power, and he'd get it—nothing less than the complete surrender of the world's governments to his authority.

Since the beginning of time kings, shoguns, emperors and generals had struggled to rule the world. From Genghis Khan to Stalin, Cyrus the Great to Napoleon, the vast armies of the world, numbering hundreds of thousands of fighting men, had fought to control all. None had succeeded.

And now, with less than two hundred active warriors, he was going to accomplish that age-old dream.

Musashi's eyes popped open as a burst of anxiety shot through his chest. His situation was fragile—all of his eggs in one basket, as the Americans said.

He was nothing without that one, deadly weapon. The realization hurt his pride.

A thin line of sweat broke out on the JRA leader's forehead. But what if the worst *did* happen? What if he should somehow lose his weapon?

No. It was impossible at this stage of the game. He'd planned too well. His eggs weren't really in one basket—they were spread across the world.

The storage bases were too diverse. They couldn't all be eliminated. A few of the locations might be discovered and destroyed—two already had been—but it would make no difference. There was no possible way for them all to be located in the time that remained. And it would take only one successful dump to realize this new dream.

Musashi closed his eyes once more. He breathed deep through his diaphragm, concentrating on each breath. Gradually the anxiety began to subside.

He bolted upright on the mat as the buzzer sounded in the wall. Pushing the button, he spoke into the screen. "Yes?"

Yuji's voice sounded hollow in the Doomsday room. "The call from America. It's urgent."

DR. TOSHIRO TAKAHATA turned as the door creaked open on rusty hinges. He saw Musashi, dressed in some sort of karate or judo costume, stick his head through the opening and scan the lab.

Against the far wall both guards jerked to attention. "Work!" one of the men said for their leader's benefit.

Takahata returned his attention to the petri dish before him. Slowly he poured a thick pink substance from the test tube onto the agar in the dish, then covered it with the lid. From the corner of his eye he saw Musashi close the door.

The old man felt the eyes of one of the guards on him. Frowning, as if in deep concentration, he slid the petri dish under a microscope and braced his arms on the table. Slowly he lowered his eye to the lens as the pain shot from his lower back down his legs.

With a short nod Takahata pushed himself erect and walked to the desk. The sharp pains in his legs returned as he bent to sit. The guard's eyes still followed his movements, so he reached for the notebook on the desktop.

As his hand touched the notebook, the bandage on Takahata's little finger brushed against the spiral wire that bound the pages. He cried out—more in shock than pain—as the exposed nerve endings sent needles piercing up his arm.

The guard who'd been watching him snickered. The other man looked up. The first guard raised his own little finger and pointed toward Takahata. Both men laughed.

Takahata stared at them for a moment, his disgust almost more than he could bear. They were not only barbarous, they were morons—as immature as ten-year-olds howling at jokes of urine and feces. They found the suffering of others humorous. He cast a final glance their way. Sometimes he wondered if the two guards even belonged to the same species as other men.

But although their witlessness had hurt him, it had aided him, as well. His two watchdogs hadn't been difficult to deceive.

Frowning once more, Takahata began scribbling nonsense equations in the notebook. He glanced up periodically, dramatically lowering his eyebrows each time and staring at the petri dish.

Slowly the old man stood and walked to the row of cages against the wall. Inside, the white rats played happily, unaware of the fate that awaited them. He watched the animals, painfully aware that they'd been his only friends since he'd arrived in this underground prison. A pang of sorrow sliced through his heart as he realized that another of the furry little beings would have to die that day. He hated the unnecessary taking of life in any form.

But was it unnecessary? No. The deaths of the rats served to deceive both the guards and Musashi himself. However unpleasant, it was imperative that he inject another rat with . . . something. He'd mix something later. Something that would kill the animal instantly—painlessly.

The old man returned to his chair and began scribbling again, glancing from the rats back to the petri dish. Suddenly an unwarranted amusement gripped his soul, threatening to make him cry out in laughter. It was as if he had reached the breaking point, absorbed all the stress and tension he could take, and some psychological, self-preservative "pop-off" valve had kicked open to prevent him from cracking.

Takahata laughed inwardly, struggling to conceal his newfound good spirits from the guards. Then, before he could stop himself, he took a final glance at the petri dish and wrote in the notebook: *There is little change. But, of course, what can one expect when one pours liquid dishwashing detergent over agar and covers the dish?*

Takahata closed the notebook. He'd continue the charade as long as necessary. He'd pour dishwashing detergent, saltwater—anything at all—into the dishes and test tubes for as long as he had to, hoping and praying with every ridiculous mixture that he'd be located and rescued.

He'd do whatever he had to do to keep the truth from Ichiro Musashi.

What he wouldn't do was reveal that he'd discovered the cure for Viryphus hours ago.

"WE WERE the first warriors to set foot on these islands," Harry said. "A hell of a long time before the word *samurai* was ever heard. We're going with you."

Bolan looked at the man standing outside the hut. Harry still wore his cowboy hat and boots, and he'd added two more effects to his Western wardrobe. A single-action Ruger Blackhawk rested in a hand-tooled quick-draw rig on his hip. Cradled in his arms was a lever-action Winchester .30-30.

Behind Harry stood six more Ainu men dressed in skins and bark-cloth and carrying a variety of swords and clubs.

Bolan looked at the first man. "What's your name?"

The man smiled self-consciously and shrugged his shoulders.

Harry started to speak, but Bolan stopped him. "Don't bother. Do any of them speak English?"

"No," Harry said. "Just me."

"Then you're the only one who goes. We won't have time for translation once it hits the fan. Besides, I'm not interested in sending men with sticks up against submachine guns and assault rifles." He glanced at Harry's outdated weaponry. "You're on limited duty, as well."

Harry shrugged and told the men. Disappointment covered the bearded faces as they turned and walked away.

Bolan didn't let it bother him. Taking them with him to fight Musashi's people would be equivalent to killing them himself. And while he could always use another trained gun, the Executioner didn't know how well Harry could shoot his primitive arms. In the long run the Ruger and Winchester wouldn't fare much better than the swords and clubs of the other Ainu.

On the other hand, the man had helped them, and the Executioner had no intention of humiliating him in front of his people. He'd find a safe place for Harry to stand guard and leave him there.

Bolan swung the Uzi over his shoulder, adjusting the sling against the stretchy material of his black combat skinsuit. He turned to Platinov. The KGB agent was dressed similarly in black pants and tunic, the thin, clinging material emphasizing every curve of her body.

Bolan grinned. The suit alone should be good for a split second of indecision on the part of any man she encountered.

The sun had fully set by the time they reached the grove of trees where they'd watched the compound earlier in the day. The Executioner pulled a night vision scope from his pack and swept the runways. Still four guards, each walking a perimeter leg under the rectangular camouflage canopy. He handed the scope to Platinov and waited while she located the men. "Take the west and south. I'll get the other two."

The Russian woman nodded.

Bolan turned to Harry. "Stay here. Guard our flank." Harry started to protest, but Bolan raised a finger to his lips. "No argument."

Bolan and Platinov sprinted from tree to tree in the relatively open terrain, finally dropping to the ground a hundred yards from the hangars. They crawled side by side for fifty more, then Bolan struck off at a forty-five-degree angle toward the east.

Stopping on his belly less than a hundred feet from the netting, he gripped the Beretta in both fists and rested his hands on the hard earth in front of him. He waited patiently until the guard passed in front, letting the moonlight behind the man silhouette his form in the darkness.

The Executioner tapped the trigger. The Beretta coughed softly in the darkness, and the passing form dropped to the ground. A second later Bolan heard a similar noise from the west as Platinov's silenced .22 did its work.

"Yoshio?" came a voice from out of the darkness. *"Doko..."* Another guard came running from the north. The man knelt next to his fallen comrade and leaned forward. Bolan squeezed the trigger once more, sending the second guard sprawling over his friend.

The Executioner leaped to his feet and sprinted toward the middle hangar. As he slid to the ground behind the brush-covered structure, he heard another soft *pffft* and a moment later Platinov stood at his side, the Woodsman gripped in her fist.

Bolan reached out for the doorknob and twisted. Locked. He turned to Platinov. "Be ready. We've got to stop them before they activate the device."

Taking a step back, the Executioner raised the Beretta and fired a single suppressed round through the tumblers. Leaping forward, he pushed through the door and raced into the hangar.

A concrete stairway led from the structure to the compound below, and the Executioner sprinted down the steps, Platinov at his heels. Jumping the last six steps to the bottom, he landed just as two shocked eyes in a bald head looked up from behind a computer. The man leaned forward, his hand reaching desperately for something on the keyboard.

Bolan raised the Beretta and added a third eye to the man's forehead. He then hurried across the room and cracked the door. Peering through, he saw one long hallway leading straight ahead. Another corridor extended to his right. To his left the tunnel ended in a concrete wall. Closing the door, he turned back to Platinov and pointed at the computer. "You're the pinball wizard. Get it on."

Bolan guarded the door, the Beretta held upright in both hands as Platinov shoved the bald man to the floor and took his seat. Sweat beaded the KGB agent's forehead as she furiously manipulated the letters and numbers on the keyboard. Five minutes went by. Then ten. Finally she looked up, smiling. "I have the code."

"Then do it," Bolan directed.

Platinov punched a series of keys and sat back, wiping the sweat from her forehead. "There, it's dismantled." The KGB agent stood up.

She'd started across the room toward Bolan when a sudden rattling sounded within the disk drive. A moment later a shrill, earsplitting alarm came from the hallway.

Platinov turned on her heels, sprinting back to the monitor. Bolan followed. Slowly, letter by letter, the words materialized on the screen: AUTOMATIC IMPULSE INTERRUPTED.

Then, in the bottom left-hand corner, ENTER CODE WORD appeared, the cursor dancing and flashing at the end of the sentence.

The Executioner stared at the monitor. COUNTDOWN typed itself tauntingly across the screen, followed by a 10 and then a 9.

Platinov gasped. "It was rigged with a fail-safe mechanism. It 'talked' back and forth to itself every few seconds." She shook her head in agony. "I didn't think of it, and I've shut down the program without going through the proper procedure, interrupting the mechanism's 'conversation' and automatically activating the dump.''

"Is there any way to divert it?" Bolan asked as the count reached four.

"Not without the code word. It has already—''

The numeral 1 appeared on the monitor, then a zero. The pulsating words and numbers vanished, and new letters emerged on the darkened screen.

DUMP ACTIVATED.

Footsteps echoed from the hallway. Bolan turned away from the computer as the door to the barracks flew open. He raised the Beretta, firing 3-round bursts into both of the JRA gunners who lunged through the door. Two subguns fell to the floor, followed by the terrorists.

Through the open door Bolan saw more men racing down the hall toward the Doomsday room. He turned back to Platinov. "Find out where the dump is,'' he shouted above the ringing alarm. "I'll hold them off.'' He charged forward, slamming the door.

The Executioner moved to the side of the door as rounds flew through the aged wood, sending splinters raining across the room. He shoved the Beretta into his shoulder holster and raised the Uzi on the end of the sling, firing his own blind rounds back through the door into the hallway. He heard a grunt outside, then a body hit the concrete.

Bolan stepped in front of the door and kicked, slivers of wood falling from the frame as it swung open. He ducked back to the side as more rounds flew through into the Doomsday room.

Platinov ducked under the onslaught and came up holding her Chinese Kalashnikov. Bolan dropped to his knees and leaned around the doorway, firing up from the unexpected angle and into the chest of a man with another Chinese AK. He cut loose two more long bursts of fire, then ducked back into the room, jamming a fresh mag into the Uzi as Platinov's pistol returned fire.

The Executioner leaned forward once more, the Uzi jerking in his hand. He sent two short bursts into a terrorist in camous who raced down the corridor to the right. The surprised man opened his mouth as if to speak. A river of red poured forth instead and he slumped to the floor.

Far down the corridor Bolan saw a man wearing three swords over his *gi* top and *hakama* pants burst into the hallway. The long, skirtlike trousers hid the man's steps, creating the illusion that he had floated into the corridor.

Platinov's eyes rose above the sights of her rifle. "That's him!" she cried. "That's Musashi!"

Bolan jumped in front of the door and swung the Uzi to his right. The corridor was clear except for the bodies littering the floor. He turned back toward Musashi just as the JRA leader jerked an older man through the door. Musashi drew a long, red-handled knife from his belt and pressed the edge of the blade against the old man's throat. "Hold your fire, Belasko-san. Unless you care to see Doctor Takahata butchered like a pig."

Bolan sighted down the barrel, trying to draw a bead on the smirking face behind Takahata. As the front sight fell on Musashi's forehead, another burst of automatic fire sounded from down the hall to his right, the rounds pounding against the concrete to his side and forcing him back into the Doomsday room.

Waiting two counts, he then leaned through the door, firing down the corridor to his right. From the corner of his eye he saw Musashi sprint away down the hall, Takahata in tow.

The warrior fired a long burst down the hall, dropping another man wearing a Rising Sun headband. He turned back to the hallway in front of him in time to see Musashi and Takahata disappear around a corner. He returned to Platinov. "Find the location of the dump," he shouted. "Then find where the other storage bases are and notify the President."

The KGB agent nodded. Dropping the AK-47 onto the floor, she slid back into the chair, her fingers moving fleetly across the keys.

Bolan sprinted to the end of the corridor, pausing briefly at the corner, and risked a quick look. Seeing nothing, he bolted around the concrete and raced on.

From somewhere ahead in the winding labyrinth of underground barracks came the steady tap of running feet. The Executioner rounded the next corner and ran smack into two more JRA gunners sprinting toward him. The two smaller men fell backward onto the floor, their eyes glazed from the impact. Bolan took them out of play with a quick burst from the Uzi.

The footsteps ahead were louder now. Bolan rounded the next corner and scanned the hall. At the far end he saw Musashi and Takahata waiting as a large concrete portal swung open. The Executioner turned on the steam, arms pumping as he raced down the narrow corridor. Still a hundred feet from the end, he saw the two men step through and the door begin to close. He was fifty feet from the portal when the door swung home. Raising his hands palm out, Bolan slammed into the door as the electronic lock clicked shut.

Above the clanking alarm, Bolan heard a voice. "Ah, Belasko-san, it seems you're a step too slow."

The Executioner looked at the wall. Mounted between the concrete blocks, he saw the intercom panel.

"I'd like to speak to you further," the voice taunted. "Explain in detail the several foolish mistakes you have made."

Bolan reached into the breast pocket of his combat suit and withdrew a claylike lump of C-4 plastique and a detonator. He began molding the plastic explosive to the door as Musashi's maniacal laughter echoed from the speaker down the hall.

"But I have a plane to catch," Musashi finished. The intercom clicked and went dead.

Bolan set the timer for ten seconds and jammed it into the plastique. Turning, he sprinted back down the hall, counting the seconds as he ran. When his count reached eight, the Executioner dived forward, sliding across the concrete, his hands over his ears. Behind him, he heard the muffled explosion and then the concussion pushed him forward, increasing the speed of his slide.

He scrambled to his feet and turned to see the door in shambles. Concrete dust and smoke floated through the air. Dashing back across the chips of gravel, he crossed the portal and raced toward the steps. From above came the sound of a small-engine plane leaving the hangar.

The Executioner bounded up the staircase and through the open door to the runway. Thirty yards ahead he saw the running lights of a Cherokee 6 as it raced along the runway.

The Executioner grimaced, running, hoping to catch the plane before it picked up speed. Arms and legs pumping like pistons, he slowly closed the gap. Twenty yards. Ten. Five.

The warrior drew the Desert Eagle as he ran, then slid it back into the holster. A well-placed shot would stop the plane's takeoff, but it might just as easily wreck the small craft, killing Takahata and the only chance the world might have left.

No, his only chance was to reach the plane before it left the ground and fight his way into the cabin.

Somehow.

The Executioner was two yards behind the Cherokee and reaching forward for the tail when the plane picked up speed, slowly widening the gap once more. By the time it reached the end of the runway and left the ground, it was forty yards ahead.

Bolan slowed to a jog as he watched the Cherokee skirt from under the canopy and rise higher into the air. Slowly the running lights—and the hopes of the world—faded into the darkness.

10

It took Platinov ten minutes to find the code. Sporadic gunfire still echoed down the corridors as she twisted in her seat and turned on the printer. Blocking the nerve-frazzling chime of the alarm from her brain, she punched the key and ran a hard copy of the twenty Viryphus storage bases spread across the globe.

Platinov turned back to the keyboard. Her fingers flew across the keys once more as she called the computer's file listing to the screen. Her eyes burned as they scrutinized the index. Dozens of the hundreds of one- and two-word codes looked promising and any of them might be the key to the automatic dump site.

The alarm still clamored as she started at the top, systematically trying each code that looked probable and keeping mental inventory of those she skipped in the event that she had to start over.

A third of the way down through the seemingly endless list she came to the word DAITO. The KGB agent's mind raced. Somewhere she had heard the term—what did it mean?

Sword Big Sword.

Platinov brought the cursor down the screen to the word, hit the retrieve key and sat back to wait. A sudden flash of movement to her side broke the Russian woman's attention. She turned toward the movement as a thin woman wearing green army fatigues flew through the door, a *kubrikiri* knife gripped tightly in her hand.

Platinov ducked, her face smashing into the keyboard as the woman screamed and swung the blade toward her neck in a wide, sweeping arc. Leaning forward onto the console, the KGB agent braced both arms and lashed out with a side kick to the woman's knee.

The woman cried out as the kick skidded across her thigh, missing the vulnerable joint. She brought down the *kubrikiri* in a vicious overhand strike. Platinov ducked to the side. The blade passed an inch from her ear, then embedded itself in the console next to the keyboard.

As the woman struggled to pry the weapon loose, Platinov shot from the chair, her hand ripping the squeeze-cocker from her side. A quick backfist from the woman sent her staggering back, the H&K flying from her hand to the floor.

Platinov lunged forward, driving a shoulder into the skinny woman's ribs. A shrill scream echoed through the room as the frail bones snapped. Platinov drove the green-clad woman to her back on the floor and scrambled on top.

All five fingers spread, Platinov struck for the eyes. The woman turned her face at the last instant, and the KGB agent's hand glanced off the side of her face. Reaching up, the woman in the fatigues launched her own eye strike.

Platinov jerked her head, avoiding the razorlike fingernails that threatened to blind her. As she moved, the woman beneath her followed the momentum, breaking the KGB agent's balance and throwing her to the side.

The Japanese woman struggled on top, pinning Platinov's arms under her knees. Bony fists pummeled down in lightning-fast strikes against the KGB agent's face, then viselike talons gripped her hair, pulling at the roots.

Platinov reached up, her thumbs finding the woman's throat. The Japanese rolled to her side, pulling Platinov with her. Over and over they rolled, first one, then the other on top, each struggling to gain control.

Like some giant human wheel, the women spun over the body of the bald man and came to a crashing halt against the wall, Platinov's hair still gripped in the other woman's claws. The KGB agent saw a crazed hunger in the eyes blazing above her as the green-clad woman's hands ripped at her tunic.

Platinov wrapped one arm around the woman's back, pinning the wiggling form to her chest. Her other hand clenched into a fist. The KGB agent extended the first joint of her index finger and brought the sharp knuckle in hard against the cracked ribs of the other woman.

Over and over Platinov repeated the strike, the knuckle digging deeper, splintering the fragile bones as the woman in green's arms thrashed impotently overhead, her screams drowning out the overhead alarm until she finally passed out.

Exhausted, the Russian woman gripped the edge of the console, struggled to her feet, then collapsed into the chair in front of the monitor. She closed her eyes, her breath coming in short, jerky gasps as her body struggled to replenish the shortage of oxygen. As her head cleared, she turned toward the computer screen.

Amid an explanatory paragraph about the automatic dump, two words flashed up to meet her eyes: ENID, OKLAHOMA.

Platinov reached for the phone, the fogginess leaving her brain. Rostipovitch. The colonel had ordered her to call him first.

She paused, the receiver halfway to her ear. There wasn't time. Already the Viryphus disease was entering the water system in... Where was it? She glanced back at the screen. Enid, Oklahoma.

Platinov pressed the phone to her ear and tapped the numbers Bolan had given her. "Mr. President," she said excitedly as the line connected, "this is Major Platinov."

"Where's Bo—Where's Belasko?"

"He's after Musashi even as we speak. Listen, please, we must hurry. The automatic dump has been activated in Enid, Oklahoma."

There was a short pause on the other end. "Where the hell is Enid, Oklahoma?" the President asked. "Never mind. We'll find it."

Platinov grabbed the paper listing the rest of the viral storage supplies. One by one she read them off.

"Tell Belasko that the special op units will strike immediately," the President said. "And I'll inform your president."

"Thank you," Platinov said. "I'm sorry. I must go."

"Certainly," the President answered. "And God go with you." Platinov heard him take a deep breath. "God go with us all."

The KGB agent set the phone back in the cradle and turned toward the door. The gunfire had stopped sometime during her fight with the woman who now lay dead at her feet. Wherever Belasko was it was too late for her to be of any help. Hesitantly she picked up the phone once more and dialed the number.

Moments later, an anxious voice answered. "Yes?"

"Colonel," she said, "it's Platinov."

"Of course it is! Who else would it be? Where are you, Major?"

"We're on Hokkaido. The main compound has been located and destroyed, but the viral-typhus disease has been released in—"

Rostipovitch interrupted. "Is the American dead?"

Fatigue engulfed Platinov as she suddenly saw Rostipovitch in a new light. His priorities had become totally distorted. He cared more about Belasko's murder than the fate of the world, which now rested in the American's hands. Irritated, she fought to control her voice. "No," she said. "Colonel, we—"

Rostipovitch's voice screamed over the line. "You have disobeyed direct orders, Major! You are to eliminate the American immediately. Now! Before he gets this disease and—"

Complete and total outrage pulled the major to her feet. "No!" she shouted back into the receiver. "I will not kill him!"

The line clicked and went dead.

Platinov sat back down in the chair, the weariness overcoming her once more. She stared at the phone in her hand, a deep, hollow emptiness creeping through her.

With that click of the phone she had lost something. How much, she couldn't know yet. Perhaps her job. Conceivably she might even be tried as a traitor to the Soviet Union.

Regardless of how serious her failure to obey orders was considered, she had at least lost Rostipovitch's friendship and respect.

The KGB agent lifted the squeeze-cocker from the console, rose from the chair and stepped over the bodies on the floor to the door. She stared down the hallway where Belasko had disappeared. She *had* lost something. But she'd gained something, as well.

Shoving the squeeze-cocker back into her holster, Marynka Platinov raced down the hall to find her partner.

A COLD, DARK FURY raced through the old man's veins as he slammed the phone onto his desk. He leaned back against the chair. The coolness of the vinyl against his sweat-soaked shirt sent shivers running down his back, and the erratic vibrations in his chest returned with a new intensity.

Rotislav Rostipovitch rose from behind the desk and walked slowly to the door, slipping the lock. Returning to his seat, he pulled the half-empty bottle of vodka from the bottom drawer of the filing cabinet. Tilting it, he drank directly from the bottle, feeling the tremors slowly dissipate as the cold, burning liquid warmed his insides.

Rostipovitch replaced the bottle in the drawer. He sat back again, gently massaging the painful muscles in his shoulders and arms. Platinov had no intention of killing the American. She had sold her soul. She had sold out her country.

She *was* in love with Belasko.

White-hot hatred enveloped him, driving the vodka's burn from his stomach. The colonel closed his eyes. The crazy, zigzag fibrillation in his chest returned. He breathed slowly, shallowly, and the shudders subsided.

Rostipovitch leaned for the phone. "Get me the president immediately," he told his secretary, and sat back again.

He breathed deeply as he waited, fighting to clear his brain of the alcohol. A moment later he heard the ring and Ivanna said, "I have his secretary on the line."

Then there was a series of clicks, and another feminine voice said, "Yes, Colonel Rostipovitch?"

"I must speak to the president immediately."

"One moment."

Rostipovitch waited, wishing he had drunk less of the vodka. He'd need a clear head for what he was about to do. The next few moments might decide the fate of the Soviet Union. Perhaps he, single-handedly, would be the one who saved the USSR from extinction.

Rostipovitch's mind drifted. He saw a statue of himself in Red Square. People surrounded it, pointing up— "Yes, Rotislav?" The voice on the other end startled him from his fantasy. "What is it?"

"Comrade," Rostipovitch said, "I've just spoken to Major Platinov. She has located and destroyed Musashi's base, but the American attempted to kill her. He has escaped with a supply of the viral-bacteria—"

"Rotislav, stop!" The president interrupted. "Before the hole you're digging for yourself becomes deeper, I must tell you that the President and I have been in constant contact throughout this crisis. Major Platinov has just called *him*."

Rostipovitch felt nausea building. He remained silent.

"She had a much different story than you now tell," the president continued. "Yes, Musashi's compound had been located and destroyed. The other storage sites have been pinpointed, as well, and even as we speak they're being neutralized by a joint operation of Spetznaz and other special units around the world."

"Comrade, I did not—"

"Be quiet and let me finish. Platinov, *and the American agent,* also discovered some type of automatic device that dumped the disease into the water system in—" he paused, and Rostipovitch heard papers rustling "—someplace called Enid, Oklahoma. The President is making efforts to control that situation, as well. Platinov and Belasko are on their way to assist. So before you hang yourself further..." The president's voice trailed off, then returned, softer. "Rotislav, we've been friends for thirty years. But the time for your way of thinking has ended. Go home, Comrade. Have a glass of vodka—if you haven't done so already—and go to sleep."

"But, Comrade—"

"You're relieved of your command, Colonel. Go home." The president paused. "Report to my office at ten o'clock tomorrow morning."

Rostipovitch heard the line go dead. He gripped the receiver in his fist, holding it away from his face, staring blankly at the slick black plastic. A new dizziness clouded his brain. Reaching into his coat, he produced the bottle and dropped two of the tiny tablets into his mouth, holding them tightly under his tongue as the receiver shook in his hand.

The shaking stopped as the nitroglycerin took effect. Ten o'clock tomorrow. At ten o'clock tomorrow it would become official.

He would lose both Marynka Platinov *and* his country.

Rostipovitch heard a series of clicks, then a dial tone replaced the silence of the instrument in his hand. He punched the intercom button and returned the receiver to his ear.

"Yes, Colonel?" Ivanna's voice sounded far away.

"Arrange for my car. Notify the airport that I'm on my way."

"Destination, Comrade Colonel?"

"I'll tell the pilot when I arrive." He slid open the top right-hand drawer of his desk and palmed the blue

Tokarev automatic. "And, Ivanna, arrange for a diplomatic pouch in my name."

"Yes, Comrade Colonel."

Rostipovitch stood shakily and walked to the mirror in the corner of his office. With trembling hands he straightened his tie. He stared into the glass, his eyes focusing fuzzily on the lines, the wrinkles, the brown liver spots on the cheeks and forehead of the face that looked back at him.

Rostipovitch turned away. He pulled his overcoat from the closet and walked toward the door.

Ten o'clock in the morning. It wouldn't become official until then.

Perhaps he still had time.

THE WHEELS OF THE B-1B hit the tarmac. As Grimaldi slowed the aircraft, Bolan watched the flashing red lights of a marked sheriff's unit at the end of the runway. Greg Hart and a man wearing a navy blue blazer and khaki slacks stood by the open car door as Bolan and Platinov stepped down from the plane.

"Belasko and Platinov," Hart told the other man as they entered the back seat. He looked at Bolan, indicating the driver with a quick snap of his head. "This is Garfield County Chief Criminal Deputy Ned Smith."

Bolan and Platinov shook hands with the deputy. Hart took the shotgun seat, and Smith pulled the car away from the runway onto the streets of Vance Air Force Base. "Bring me up to date," Bolan said.

"Basically we're at a standstill. Air Force personnel and soldiers from Fort Sill—that's south of here in

Lawton—have cordoned off the city. The highways and all back roads have been shut off."

"When?" Platinov asked.

"The quarantine went into effect three hours after you called, ma'am." Hart twisted, resting an elbow over the seat and looking momentarily at the Russian woman. He turned to Bolan. "Doctor von Studnitz is here. They've located the spot where the disease was dumped into the reservoir. It had time to get into the main tank, but he doesn't think it could have entered the private lines before the city was closed off. Anyone who left town before the military got set up should be safe."

As they approached the gate, a security police officer stepped down from the guard shack, saluted and waved them through. Smith glanced up into the rearview mirror, peering at their reflections through his steel-framed glasses. "Command post has been set up at the sheriff's office," he said. "Fifteen-minute drive."

They pulled out onto a thin strip of blacktop, then onto a long, curving drive leading into the city. As they neared an access road leading onto the main highway into town, Bolan saw a convoy of troop carriers making their way slowly along the road.

"Shit," Smith said. He leaned forward, flipping a switch on the dash, and Bolan saw the red lights on the roof flash on. "Troops have been coming in all morning." The deputy pulled into the oncoming lane and passed the convoy.

"Any word on Musashi?" Bolan asked.

A flicker of confusion flashed over Hart's face. "No, not that I've heard. He could be anywhere." The Secret Service agent frowned. "Why? You think he'd come here?"

"With an ego like his, yeah," Bolan said. "I don't think the man will be able to stay away. He'll have to see his master plan in action."

Hart nodded. "You almost got him, I understand. Would you recognize him now?"

Bolan shook his head. "He was too far away."

They rode down the highway in silence, Smith slowing to a crawl at each stoplight before hitting his siren briefly and shooting through. Enid looked like a town under siege as they turned right on Main and made their way through a residential section. Jeeps, troop carriers and government vehicles of every type seemed to cover each block. As they reached the downtown square, they saw National Guard troops occupying deserted retail buildings that surrounded the courthouse and post office.

Smith shook his head. "Big mall went in on the west side of town a few years ago. Most of downtown here went under. Pawn shops are about all that survived." A wry grin curled the corners of his mouth. "Nobody realized the empty space would come in handy some day."

The deputy made a U-turn in front of the courthouse and pulled into a parking spot marked Police and Highway Patrol. He jumped out, opening the door for Platinov before leading them toward the steps of the building.

A group of young Indian men sat casually on the courthouse steps, laughing and joking as if nothing unusual was happening around them. Dressed in faded blue jeans, T-shirts and western boots, they turned toward Smith as he approached. A small man, his face partially hidden by a ragged straw cowboy hat, turned away as they approached, the long braids under the hat flipping with the movement.

A tall, lanky man with flowing black hair rose from his seat as they reached the steps. "Hey, Smith, man," he said. "I gotta talk with you."

"Not now, Paladin," Smith said as they started up the steps.

"But damn it, Ned, I gotta see my brother. He's lookin' at five to life. I can't make it up here during visiting hours—I gotta work."

"Stop at the desk and talk to Sherry," Smith replied without breaking stride. "We'll work something out."

"Thanks, man."

Smith led them into the courthouse to the elevator. They stopped in front of the green metal doors while he pressed the button marked Down. As they waited, Bolan saw Platinov staring at a large mural painted on the wall across the hall. Two mounted Indian warriors with bows and arrows chased a buffalo across the plains.

Smith smiled. "Indian artist did some time here for drunk driving a few years ago. Guy who was sheriff then liked him. Made him a trustee and let him paint. His pictures are all over the courthouse, on the walls in the jail cells, everywhere."

The doors slid open and a small elderly man wearing a bow tie leaned forward from a stool in the corner. "Come on in." He grinned, holding the control lever.

They rode one flight down, then the doors swung open again. "Thanks, Swede."

Bolan, Platinov and Hart followed the deputy down the hall and made a sharp right turn. A thin, pretty girl with freckles sat at a gunmetal-gray desk in front of a glass wall. She looked up briefly, saw Smith and pushed a button on the desk. The electronic lock in the door buzzed and Smith led them in.

The Executioner heard a loud voice booming from a side office as they followed Smith through the door. "I don't give a damn *who* you are, Brognola. This is *my* county. I'm the sheriff!"

"I've got to check in with the President," Hart said, and disappeared into another of the offices.

Bolan, Platinov and Smith stopped at the door marked Sheriff. Hal Brognola stood just inside the open door, looking up at a giant of a man. Six feet ten inches in the air, a prematurely gray head glared down at the Justice man. A Smith & Wesson Chief's Special hung from the sheriff's belt, looking like a toy on the three-hundred-pound frame.

A short man with a Clark Gable mustache and a military bearing stood next to Brognola. He spoke softly to the giant.

Smith turned to Bolan and grinned. "Don't worry about the sheriff. Undersheriff'll quiet him down. He always does." The short man continued to talk, and the sheriff's scowl relaxed.

Smith rapped on the door frame and Brognola turned. A smile of relief covered the Justice man's face as his eyes fell on Bolan. The expression faded as the knowledge of the Executioner's fate obviously returned to his mind. He walked from the office to the hall and extended his hand. "Striker."

"Fill me in," Bolan said. "But first, have you found the leak to Musashi?"

Brognola shook his head. "Not yet."

"What's the situation here?"

Brognola hooked a thumb back toward the sheriff's office. "What you just saw in there is only the tip of the iceberg. We've got a city that's about to explode."

Footsteps sounded in the hallway on the other side of the glass, and Bolan turned to see that some of the Indians from the steps had followed them in and were talking to the receptionist. Smith opened the door, stuck his head through and said, "Sherry, work some kind of jail visitation out for Paladin."

Bolan turned back to Brognola. "Go on, Hal."

Brognola started to continue when a door opened on the other side of the hall. Dr. von Studnitz appeared and walked to Brognola's side.

"Give him the technical rundown, Doctor," the Justice man said.

Von Studnitz played nervously with the knot in his tie. "For the time being, at least, the disease has been contained within the city. The quarantine was established quickly before the viral-bacteria had a chance to enter the water lines leading to private consumption." He pulled a white handkerchief from his lapel pocket and dabbed at his forehead. "But no one thought to simply shut down the water supply at that point. By the time it *was* closed off, I'm certain the Viryphus disease had ample time to work into the pipes."

"This is your field of expertise," Bolan told him. "What's your plan of attack?"

Von Studnitz shook his head. "I don't know. We're at a standstill. The only possible way to neutralize the Viryphus threat at this point is the discovery of an antitoxin that can be added to the water system and run through on top of the disease itself. That could take months . . . years. In the meantime—"

Bolan frowned. "You said before that Doctor Takahata was close to the antitoxin."

"Yes, but that was Doctor Takahata. He's months ahead in his research. But we don't know where he is, and without his help, or even his notes . . . I just don't know."

Brognola broke in. "In the meantime, Striker, no one in the city can leave. The President's ruled Enid a national disaster area. Drinking water's being hauled in. But it'll never be enough. Can you imagine what'll happen in the streets when it begins to run out?"

Hart came out of the side office. He pointed at the portable transistor phone in his hand. "The President," he said. "Any changes to report?"

Brognola shook his head. "Just tell him Belasko and Platinov have arrived." The big Fed turned back to Bolan. "We've put the news on TV and radio. National Guardsmen, police, Oklahoma State Bureau of Investigation agents, everybody we can round up is going door-to-door to warn people not to drink from their taps. But they'll miss somebody. They're bound to. And sooner or later we're going to have a carrier running around giving Viryphus to everyone." The Justice man stopped abruptly and drew another long breath of air. He looked from Bolan to Platinov. "I hate to ask, Striker. But...how long before you two need to be quarantined?"

Bolan raised his wrist. "Two hours. Four o'clock."

The Justice man's shoulders slumped slightly, then straightened. "Who'd have thought it would end this way," he whispered.

Loud voices came from the hallway outside the glass. Bolan, Platinov, Smith and Brognola turned to see the Indians still there. The tall, lanky man argued with the girl behind the desk.

Just to the side of the desk Bolan saw the short Indian in the cowboy hat and braids. The man's face pressed against the glass as he stared into the Sheriff's Department. As the Executioner's eyes met his, he turned away and walked swiftly down the hall, disappearing around the corner.

Bolan felt strong fingers grip his arm. He turned to the side and saw Platinov staring at the glass. The blood had drained from her face. "I think that's him," she whispered.

"What?" Bolan asked.

"The one with the braids," Platinov answered. "I think it's Musashi."

11

Bolan was the first through the door, followed by Smith.

"Paladin," the deputy asked quickly, "who was the guy with the braids?"

The tall Indian shrugged. "Never saw him before, Ned. Probably Pawnee. Look, Sherry says I can't..."

Brognola and Platinov joined them in the hall as they rounded the corner to the closed elevator doors. "He didn't have time to get on," Bolan said. He turned to Smith. "Which way?"

Smith pointed down the hall. They sprinted across the tile and turned up a short set of steps leading back to the front lawn of the courthouse. Bolan scanned the area. His eyes fell on the braided man crossing the street to the post office building.

"Freeze!" Smith roared, drawing a Browning Hi-Power from beneath his jacket.

The man in the braids turned in the middle of the street, a nickel-plated automatic in his hands. He fired three rounds in their direction, sending the Indians who were still on the steps diving to the concrete.

Bolan heard a low moan to his side and turned to see Brognola in the grass, his foot grasped in both hands. "Go on!" the big Fed shouted. "It's not bad."

The Desert Eagle had already jumped into Bolan's hand as Musashi turned and sprinted up the steps to the post office. The Executioner leveled the sights as the JRA leader ducked behind a group of Camp Fire Girls climbing the stairs.

Pushing the girls aside, Musashi reached the top and twisted back, firing two more rounds as Bolan, Platinov and Smith sprinted after him. Musashi disappeared through the glass doors.

The Executioner took the steps three at a time, ripping the door open and diving inside. Another pair of rounds sailed over his head as he hit the tile, rolled across the lobby and came to a stop against a wall of post office boxes.

Bolan rolled back onto his stomach as another round drilled through the tiny glass window of one of the boxes. Screams came from his left, and he turned to see a dozen people break line in front of the mailing counter, falling to the ground in a tangle of bodies, steel posts and red velvet separation rope. Just beyond the confusion a door to the outside swung closed.

The Executioner sprang to his feet as Smith and Platinov entered the post office. He heard their feet clatter after him as he raced to the door, vaulting the horrified people who had ducked under the shots.

Bursting through the door, the warrior saw the braided wig on the post office steps. He raced past it as Musashi crossed the lawn and bolted across a side street toward a block of retail businesses. Ducking behind a parked car, the JRA leader fired three more rounds as the shoppers on the sidewalk froze in disbelief.

The Executioner charged forward. Musashi fired once more, and the slide of the automatic locked open. He dropped the empty weapon onto the sidewalk and drew the red-handled knife from beneath his checkered shirt.

An elderly woman in a long raincoat came walking down the sidewalk, a cloth-covered bowl in her hands. She appeared oblivious to what was going on around her.

The JRA leader turned as she came abreast of a plate-glass window bearing the words Little's Loans— The Pawnshop with Class.

He bolted across the sidewalk and wrapped an arm around the old woman's neck. The steaming bowl fell to the pavement as he pressed the edge of the knife against her throat.

"Stay back!" the JRA leader screamed. Pulling the woman with him, he backed slowly against the glass door.

Bolan stopped at the curb. He trained the front sights of the mammoth .44 Magnum on the man with the knife, but Musashi shrank farther behind the woman. "Stay back, Belasko-san," the JRA leader shouted. "Don't follow me inside or I'll slice her head from her body."

Musashi backed harder against the glass and the door inched open. Still holding the woman tightly, he slithered through the opening and the door swung closed.

Bolan sprinted to the door. Behind him he heard Platinov and Smith cross the street and come to a halt next to him.

Sunlight streamed through the glass to form a spotlight of dancing dust motes around the JRA man and his hostage. "Don't enter!" Musashi screamed through the glass. "I'll kill her!"

Bolan's mind raced, a dozen options speeding through his brain. In a heartbeat the Executioner appraised the plans of attack, discarding each just as fast as too uncertain.

Suddenly a shot exploded from inside the store, and Bolan saw a tiny hole appear in the glass door to his side. As he pushed through the door, the Executioner saw the old woman twist away from Musashi and flee behind a glass counter against the wall.

Musashi stared at Bolan as he entered the shop, his face a mask of astonishment. The knife fell from his hand, and then the JRA leader dropped to his knees on the carpet.

Behind Musashi Bolan saw a stocky man with brown hair graying at the temples. A stainless-steel S&W Model 66 extended from his outstretched hand.

Musashi held his abdomen with one hand and leaned forward, reaching for the knife with the other. The big .44 bucked in the Executioner's fist, the round striking the floor next to the knife. Musashi's hand jerked back as the blade skipped to the side.

"Move again and I'll kill you," Bolan growled. "Where's Takahata?"

Blood poured from the JRA leader's gut wound. A vile scowl replaced the shock on his face. A trickle of crimson ran from the corner of his mouth as he spoke. "I'll never tell you."

Bolan walked forward and pressed the Desert Eagle against Musashi's forehead. "Then you'll die."

A hideous cackle escaped the terrorist's throat. "I'll die, anyway. But I'll make you a deal."

"No deals. Where's Takahata?"

"I don't ask for freedom," Musashi said. "I'll tell you what you wish to know if you'll allow me to die as the samurai that I am." His head indicated the knife on the floor. "Allow me to commit seppuku, the death of the warrior."

Bolan stepped back, the big automatic still trained on the JRA leader. "You're not a warrior. You're a weak coward who hides behind women and old men." He dropped the Desert Eagle to his side. "But tell me where he is and you'll die as you wish."

Musashi reached forward, grasping the handle of the weapon with blood-streaked fingers. "Before I give you his location I'll tell you something else of interest. The old man talks in his sleep. On the flight from Hokkaido I learned that he's discovered the cure for the disease."

"My patience is running thin." Bolan raised the .44 once more. "Where is he?"

"He has the antitoxin, Belasko-san," Musashi sneered. "But you won't have him!" Twisting the blade in his hands, he plunged it toward his abdomen.

Two .44 magnums from the Desert Eagle beat the blade.

BOLAN DROPPED to one knee and dug through Musashi's pockets as Platinov and Smith walked into the shop.

"Son of a bitch, you cut it close, Captain," Smith said. He turned to the gray-templed man who was helping the elderly lady from behind the counter. "That round wasn't exactly in the X-ring. You getting rusty since retirement?"

"Up yours, Smittie," the retired Captain Little said. "I always said I'd gut-shoot any bastard who fucked with my mother." The elderly woman frowned at him, and Little reddened. "Sorry about the language, Mom."

Bolan pulled a motel key from Musashi's jeans and held it up to the light. Room 127—Trail Motel, it read on the chipped plastic ring. "Captain," he said, "call the sheriff's office. There's a man there by the name of von Studnitz. Tell him to get a lab set up somewhere. He can radio us as to the location in Smith's unit." He rose from the floor. "You know where the Trail is, Smith?"

"Sure."

"Let's go."

Bolan, Platinov and Smith sprinted out the door as two city police cars pulled to a halt in front of Little's. Smith waved them inside as they darted across the street and then crossed back to the front of the courthouse.

Hart came running down the steps as they reached Smith's car. "Little just called. I'll go with you."

Bolan slid behind the wheel with Smith at his side. Platinov and Hart climbed into the back seat. The

Executioner twisted the key and revved the engine. "Point me in the right direction," he told Smith.

Lights flashing and siren blaring, Bolan pushed the sheriff's car through the streets. Just before they reached the highway they'd come in on, Smith directed him into the parking lot of a deserted bank building. They crossed the lot, jumped the curb and entered the motel lot from the rear.

Bolan skidded the car to a halt in front of the pool, leaped from behind the wheel and raced toward room 127. Without breaking stride the Executioner kicked the door and burst through to see an elderly Oriental man lying on the bed, his hands and feet bound with adhesive tape.

Bolan cut the restraints from the old man while Platinov pulled the strip of tape from his mouth. "Doctor Takahata?" she asked.

The man sat up stiffly, rubbing his back. He swung both feet over the bed to the floor and nodded.

"Doctor," Bolan began, "we've got to work fast. We're setting up a—"

A short, pudgy woman with half-glasses hanging from a chain around her neck came stalking angrily into the room. She looked directly at Hart and said, "Mr. Johnson, what on God's green earth is—"

"Police emergency, ma'am," Hart said quickly, grabbing the woman by the arms and pushing her back toward the door. "You'll have to wait outside."

The woman struggled, breaking free. "Show me a badge," she demanded. "Mr. Johnson, when I rented you the room this morning I had no idea that this sort of thing—"

Hart grabbed the woman again. "You've got me confused with somebody else." He pushed her roughly through the opening and slammed the door in her face.

When the agent turned around again, he was staring down the bores of a Desert Eagle, a Browning Hi-Power and an H&K squeeze-cocker. Bolan yanked the pistol from Hart's holster as Smith shoved the man's face into the wall. The deputy pulled a set of handcuffs from his belt and secured the Secret Service man's wrists behind his back. "Wait a minute," Hart sputtered. "I can explain this. I—"

Smith jerked the cuffs upward and Hart cried out in pain.

"We'll be happy to listen to whatever shit you come up with," the deputy said, "later. Right now we've got to clean up your mess." He opened the door and launched the Secret Service man through.

Bolan helped Takahata to his feet and into the car as another Sheriff's Department vehicle came tearing into the parking lot from the highway. The big sheriff squeezed through the driver's door as Brognola limped from the passenger seat, a red-splattered towel wrapped around his ankle.

Bolan grabbed Hart's cuffs and propelled him toward the sheriff, who caught the man as if he were a rag doll. "Here's the leak, Hal. You okay?"

Brognola nodded. "Just a scratch." He looked at Hart, shook his head, then turned back to Bolan. "Von Studnitz has set up shop in the science building at Phillips University. On the other side of town— about ten minutes." He glanced at his watch. "You don't take orders well, Striker. But I want you to take this one. As soon as they've manufactured enough of the antitoxin, I want you and Platinov to be the first injected. Understand?'' Without waiting for an answer he turned to Takahata. ''These two have been exposed to Viryphus, Doctor. They've got less than an hour before their seventy-two are up.''

Takahata's eyes widened. ''But assuming von Studnitz has already arranged things, it will take me some time—''

''Then get on it,'' the Justice man growled. He grabbed Hart by the lapels and threw him into the back seat as the sheriff bent double and stuffed himself back behind the wheel.

Bolan threw the keys to Smith. ''You know the way. You drive.'' He helped Takahata into the passenger's seat and slid into the back next to Platinov.

Smith hit both lights and siren and pulled onto the highway.

The Executioner felt Platinov's hand find his.

VON STUDNITZ WAS setting up equipment and giving orders to several college chemistry students and a professor when they arrived.

Bolan and Platinov settled into wooden desks at the side of the laboratory as Takahata took charge. Von Studnitz joined the others, scurrying off to cupboards and sinks and returning with items the Japanese scientist ordered.

The warrior saw Platinov glance nervously at the round white-faced clock on the wall as the seconds ticked away. She turned to him, a weak smile on her lips. "It'll be close," she whispered.

Bolan smiled back. Over the past few days he'd grown to like the Russian woman. And since the incident in the Ainu hut with the granola bar, he'd learned to trust her. The KGB agent was a professional, doing her job as best she could within the restrictions that governed her and her own personal limitations.

Perhaps more importantly, she was a good, honest and moral human being who'd risked her life to save the rest of the world. No one could ask more of a person than that.

Bolan reached over, taking her hand in his. "You know what Yogi Berra used to say."

A puzzled look covered the Russian woman's face. "You're about to quote a cartoon bear?"

Bolan chuckled. "No, a baseball player. 'It ain't over till it's over.'"

Platinov looked puzzled. "That's obvious, isn't it?" She shook her head. "There's much about you Americans I still don't understand." She squeezed his hand. "I'm afraid, Belasko."

"It's almost over."

She nodded. "Yes, I suppose so. One way or the other it's about to end."

The hands of the clock stood at 3:54 when Takahata finally turned to them and nodded. Bolan and Platinov rose from the desks and walked forward.

"You're very close to the deadline," the old man said as he hung two clear bags of colorless liquid from IV posts. "I don't wish to take chances—we will saturate you both with the antitoxin." He motioned them toward a Formica-topped table next to the posts. "I'm sorry, but we have no beds available."

The old man inserted the needles into Bolan's and Platinov's veins, and they lay back side by side as the fluid containing the antitoxin began dripping through the plastic tubes.

Von Studnitz stood over them, smiling down. "That's what you call a photo finish."

Bolan grinned. Takahata and Platinov looked at each other, puzzled. "It has something to do with pictures?" Platinov asked.

"Never mind," von Studnitz said. "It was close." He turned to Takahata. "We'll need to set up several more manufacturing spots around town, I suppose."

The old man nodded. "It will take a great deal of the antitoxin to clear the water supply."

"I'll contact the Sheriff's Department. There are several high schools in the area. They'll all have labs. It won't take long once we're set up. The important thing is, it's now under control. I'd say we're safe."

Suddenly a shot exploded from the hallway. The track light above their heads burst into slivers of glass and rained down on the floor below.

Bolan jerked to his elbows as a husky, heavily accented voice said, "Major Platinov."

A pallid-faced man in a brown hat and overcoat stepped into the laboratory. He held a Tokarev automatic in both hands. "You have disobeyed orders."

Slowly the Executioner moved his hand toward the Beretta under his arm.

The man with the Tokarev caught the movement. "No," he ordered, swinging the gun toward Bolan.

Platinov rose to her elbows. "Colonel Rostipovitch," she pleaded. "Don't do this."

The colonel's crazed eyes bulged under the brim of the hat. Rostipovitch swung the gun back to her. "It *must* be done." The Tokarev moved again to the Executioner.

Bolan's fingers found the butt of the 93-R as Platinov rolled over on top of him, pinning his hand between them. "No!" she screamed. "Colonel...no!"

The Executioner shoved her back and drew the Beretta as Rostipovitch's eyes suddenly ballooned in the sockets. The color drained from his face, leaving it a feeble, waxen gray. The colonel's free hand shot to his chest, and he staggered back against the wall, the Tokarev rolling forward to hang upside down by the trigger guard as the fingers of his gun hand fell open.

"Marynka," he sputtered. "Marynka...I...love you."

Bolan saw the squeeze-cocker in the Russian woman's hand. Tears rolled down her cheeks as she leveled it on the colonel and spoke. "And I you, as well, Colonel Rostipovitch."

A sickly smile twisted Rostipovitch's mouth. Then he choked twice, gasping for air.

"You've been like a father to me, Colonel. Don't do this..."

Rostipovitch's chest jerked forward. He grasped the Tokarev and brought it up. The Desert Eagle barked, followed by the sharp cracks of the Tokarev and then Platinov's H&K. Colonel Rostipovitch dropped facedown on the floor.

Bolan turned to Platinov. The Russian woman lay on her back, her hand pressed against the blood that dripped from the flesh wound in her upper thigh. She smiled weakly up at the Executioner. "It's over," she said softly.

Bolan lay back and slipped an arm under her shoulders. "Yes," he replied, "it is."

Be sure not to miss Book 2 of the new action-packed series
TIME WARRIORS.

FORBIDDEN REGION
David North
THE BROTHERHOOD PACT

TEXAS—Workers at a uranium-processing
plant die suddenly, inexplicably... and in agony.
The town is declared a nuclear disaster area.
Evacuation is immediate.

THE FORBIDDEN ZONE—In a desolate area
in a parallel dimension, strange glowing rocks
have come to light. The nearby inhabitants are
dwindling in numbers.

THE AEGEAN—A mysterious figure heads
a sinister operation to depopulate
many worlds. Only two men can thwart
him: Black Jack Hogan and Brom,
Lord of Kalabria.

Destiny has joined these modern and ancient
warriors to battle a sinister power in
two worlds.

On the savage frontier of tomorrow,
survival is a brand-new game.

FROZEN FIRE
James McPhee

David Rand faces his final test—in the third book of Gold Eagle's
SURVIVAL 2000 series.

In the cruel new world created by the devastation of asteroid impacts,
Rand's family is held captive by a murderous gang of army deserters.

With a fortress established in a crumbling mall, the enemy will always
hold the high ground unless Rand can pass the test in a world where
winners die hard . . . and losers live to tell the tale.

Raw determination in
a stilborn land...

JAMES AXLER

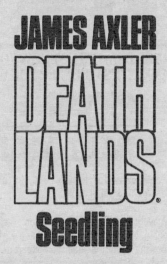

DEATH LANDS.

Seedling

As Ryan Cawdor and his roaming band of survivors desperately seek to escape their nuclear hell, they emerge from a gateway into the ruins of Manhattan.

Under this urban wasteland lives the King of the Underground, presiding over his subterranean fortress filled with pre-nuke memorabilia. And here, in this once-great metropolis, lives Ryan Cawdor's son....

The children shall inherit the earth.

TAKE 'EM FREE
4 action-packed novels plus a mystery bonus

NO RISK
NO OBLIGATION TO BUY

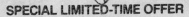